KILLER SISTER

The Complete Series
Katlin Stack
Published By Katlin Stack, 2024

I
KILLER SISTER

Chapter 1

For most people, sitting at the reading of their mother's last will and testament would feel like a nightmare.

But my nightmares had always been far more gruesome than that.

"Kylie?"

I heard my name and blinked, trying to erase the thoughts that were circulating in my mind.

"Sorry...did you say something?" I asked. One of my chronic headaches was pressing against the backs of my eyes making it harder to focus than it already was.

Mr. O'Neal, my mother's lawyer, cleared his throat. "Yes, I asked if your Aunt Cheryl was going to be joining us? Or if I should proceed without her."

His expensive gold watch glinted as he turned his chubby arm to purposefully check the time. Everything about him seemed to be too much. From his overstuffed leather chairs in his office, the stack of books with uncracked spines used only to impress people, to his tailored suit on his bulging body. He was clean and crisp, and overindulgent.

"I haven't heard from her. She got my message about Mom but she's halfway around the world photographing a shoot for some magazine, so I don't think she'll be making it here. They weren't...close."

Mr. O'Neal nodded. "Then maybe we should just get started," he said, his voice full of pity.

My eyes dropped to my lap. I didn't want his pity. I didn't want him to feel sorry for me. But what else could he think? I was just about to turn nineteen years old, technically an adult for a whole year, and I had no one. The only family I had left had just been buried. I was alone.

I guessed I would have felt bad for me too.

Mr. O'Neal began to read my mother's last will to the room.

Both her alma mater and her favorite charities were left a great deal of money, a few of her friends were left little remembrances, Aunt Cheryl was left some of the heirlooms from their family, and I was left everything else.

I may have been alone, but I was suddenly rich. Somehow, that didn't quite make up for it.

"Your mother wanted me to play this recording for you," Mr. O'Neal said. Turning on a flat screen that was mounted on the wall, my mother's face sat frozen and distraught on the screen.

He pressed play.

"To my daughter, I leave my home and the possessions not already given, the rest of the money I possessed, and a lifetime full of regret. I wish I could have been brave enough to tell you the truth while I was alive, to be better for you, to give you the love you deserved. Instead, I doubt I even told you the one thing I always wanted to say. To tell you that I'm sorry. I hope that this box will, at the very least, help you understand why life was the way it was for us. And why I failed you as a mother."

Mr. O'Neal paused the recording and handed me a locked wooden box with paint chips flaking from it. At one time there might have been flowers on the lid, but there was barely anything left. The lock's color was nearly rubbed away, having been opened too many times. My thumb rubbed the lock, where I was sure my mother's thumb had done the same.

"What's inside?" I asked.

"She didn't tell me. But...she did have the key." He handed me a necklace, one that I had seen every day for my entire life. On the chain sat a matching gold key which, up until that moment, I had always thought was just a piece of jewelry.

I snatched it from his hands. Anger mixed with something I couldn't describe bubbled inside of me. "Where did you get this?" I demanded. "I've been looking everywhere for this! I wanted her to wear it in her...her...casket," I said barely able to get the words out.

"As per her instructions, I was supposed to be called when she passed away, and I was to take the necklace from her and make sure it landed in your hands."

I started to put the key into the lock when I heard my mother's voice again.

"There is one more thing that I want to say to you, Kylie."

I looked back up to the screen and saw a small smile tug at the corners of her lips.

"You have been the only bright spot in this life. Without you, I wouldn't have lasted as long as I did. I love you, Kylie."

The screen went dark.

The room went silent.

And my first tears slid hot down my cheeks.

Chapter 2

The funeral was over, her will had been read, and the last of the sympathetic calls had come in. Now it was just me in the living room, curled into the corner of the soft blue couch that we'd had forever. The box on my lap.

I toyed with the key, twirling it through my fingers, wondering if I even wanted to open that box or not.

I didn't know what my mother was hiding but I truly wasn't sure if I even wanted to know.

Weren't secrets better left buried?

Or was knowledge power?

I doubted anything in that box was enough to change my life in any facet.

But it had to be something, why else would she keep it under literal lock and key?

After I'd flipped through every streaming service I could think of and started and stopped every murder documentary I could find, I knew that I wasn't going to be able to focus on anything until I knew what was in that box.

I stared at it, wishing somehow that I could suddenly develop x-ray vision and see inside without having to give in and open it. It was an act of defiance, I was sure, that I didn't want my mother, wherever she may be in the afterlife, to see me opening it. Somehow opening the box felt like a strange step towards forgiveness, like there may have been some reason she had kept me at arm's length for my entire life. But forgiving her wasn't something I was ready to do quite yet.

I shook a white pill out of my orange prescription bottle and popped it into my mouth. Before I swallowed it down, I savored the thought of the effects I knew it would give me. In a few minutes, I knew the blinding pain behind my eyes would ease, just like the images that were never too far away.

For a few minutes, I sat there with an opened bottle of wine, snatched from my mother's liquor cabinet. She only ever carried the best. I smiled faintly at the memories of sneaking liquor from there without her knowing. I realized I wouldn't have to sneak anything anymore.

As if with a mind of their own, my fingers jabbed the key into the lock and twisted. It popped off with a click that echoed in the quiet of the house.

My heart raced as I lifted the lid.

What could be in there that had wrecked her life so badly? And then, in turn, had damaged mine?

A letter sat on top. Perfectly folded, my name scrawled in her shaky handwriting. My fingers brushed it and I pictured her writing my name one last time in life.

I didn't pause to give the moment any kind of glory and instead ripped open the envelope.

Pulling the letter out I took a breath, wondering if I hoped for answers to explain it all or if I hoped for more excuses so that I could stay angry.

Kylie,

By now you know that there is something I've always hidden from you. And for the lies, the hurt, and all the pain, I know you can never forgive me. But if you are reading this, then I am gone, and I have no choice but to stop protecting you from the truth.

You were born a twin. Two twin girls. Two perfectly healthy, pink, beautiful baby girls. Exactly alike. Not even a freckle of a difference between you. Sometimes your father and I didn't even know how to tell you apart. We loved you both so unconditionally...and I guess that is where we got into trouble.

Your sister...while she was born physically healthy, mentally she was not quite right. It started with her screaming all night long. We ended up having to put her in a separate room from you so as not to keep you awake. Nothing ever worked. We'd feed her, change her, rock her, we even took her to the doctor many times to see if something was wrong. Nothing ever was.

Then as she grew, other things began to stand out. She would have violent temper tantrums, she would hurt you and take pleasure in it, she hurt the pets we owned and would giggle when they cried. We tried to get her evaluated but there was nothing they could find that was wrong with her. Still, the older she grew, the more concerned we became.

She became more aggressive, more dangerous, and we were so afraid one day she'd hurt herself. Or she would hurt you. And we couldn't bear the thought of that happening. We wanted her to get the help she so clearly needed so we found a nice place to send her. Holden Lake Institute. They were equipped to help children of that nature and we hoped one day she'd get better.

It killed us to make this decision. It destroyed our family. I couldn't forgive myself and while your father always blamed me for not being able to get over it, he never did look me in the eyes again. Not even as he drove away from us.

And you, Kylie, you suffered more than all of us. You lost your sister, your family, and your future that day we dropped her off.

Every month, I send a check from a private fund to which I am giving you access. All I ask is that you keep paying to keep her locked away. The money will always be there, of that you can be sure. She can never come out. After reading this letter I'm sure it's a tall order to ask but I need you to trust me.

Please, never go see her, never let her get out. I'm sorry for all I've done, for all I've put you through, and I'm sorry I brought her into this world.

I love you, Kylie. That has been my one truth in life.

Love,
Mom

Chapter 3

I must have reread that letter at least a hundred times, trying to understand it all.

I had absolutely no memory of a sister, not even an inkling. No running around playing together, no sharing toys, nothing that would have even sparked an idea that my family had ever been more than an absent father and a drunk mother. I wouldn't have even believed that it was true except for the fact that underneath the letter was proof.

There was the bank account with the account numbers and statements each month to a hospital I'd never heard of.

There were pictures, family photos of us all, the four of us. Pictures from the hospital, coming home from the hospital, us as babies in the tub. Picture after picture of the four of us, a normal family. Anyone else looking at them would have thought we were the perfect little family.

Somehow, the pictures, as real as they were, didn't feel real. The letter, the bank account, none of it seemed like it was my life. It felt like some wild dream...or maybe even a nightmare.

Then, buried at the bottom, was my sister's birth certificate. I picked it up, afraid that it might disappear right there from my hands. Suddenly, it felt real.

My sister's name was Kara.

She was born two minutes after me. Which wouldn't be so strange.

Except I was born on October 30th, at 11:58 pm.

That meant two things. One, we were twins with two separate birthdays. Two, she was born at midnight on Halloween.

Suddenly, I just couldn't sit there on the couch, in the quiet, with those pictures and lies strewn across my lap.

I jammed everything back into the box and slammed the lid. I clicked the lock back in place, put the box on the coffee table, and slid it to the far end.

I was shaking. A shake so deep inside my bones that I didn't know if I could ever make it stop. The pill wasn't helping my blinding headache, so I popped another, hoping to calm the pain and my mind.

My entire life, my family, my whole world had been a lie.

I didn't sleep a wink that night. I'm not even sure I ever closed my eyes to even try. How could I?

In one night, I'd learned that I had a secret sister locked away in an institute, I learned why my mother was an alcoholic, and why my father left. Briefly, I wondered if that's where the gaps in my memory came from...from a past I didn't want to remember.

It was all too much to handle on my own.

Not even caring what the time was over wherever she might be, I called the only person who I hoped could make sense of what I'd learned.

But true to her normal self, Aunt Cheryl didn't answer the call.

On her answering machine, I spilled everything I'd just learned. Going around in circles with the information until I finally came to a conclusion on my own.

"Aunt Cheryl, I need answers. And there is only one place that I am going to get those answers. I need to go see Kara."

As soon as I hung up the phone, I knew that that was exactly what I needed to do. I needed to go see my sister. I needed to see her for myself, to hear what she had to say and gain some understanding.

A quick search on my phone told me that it was only a couple of hours away. I would leave first thing in the morning and be there by early afternoon. After all, what else was I going to do with my time?

There was nothing else, no one else, and no reason not to go.

Chapter 4

Holden Lake Institute was nothing like the way movies depict institutions. It was clean, bright, and welcoming. The people that were sent there clearly had the money to be there. Even if my sister were as dangerous as my mother's letter described, it didn't surprise me that she would send her to an institute of luxury.

A woman at the front desk greeted me with a wide smile. "Can I help you?" she asked.

With all the non-stop thinking I'd been doing, one would have thought that I had planned out what to say to anyone once I got there, but I had no idea what I was doing.

"I...I'm here...um...my sister...I think she's here...and I...I don't really know. I guess...I'd like to see her?"

The woman tilted her head slightly and smiled. "Do you have an appointment?"

"Oh...no. I don't. Do I need one to see my own sister?"

"Yes, all visits require an appointment. Just to ensure our patients don't get overwhelmed or have other engagements."

"Engagements?"

"Classes, meetings, therapy...things like that."

I knew I must have looked like a whole lot of things. Confused, disappointed, maybe even scared.

She looked around quickly before looking back at me. "What's the patient's name?" she whispered.

"Kara Heston," I said.

The woman's eyes went wide. "You're...you're here for Kara?"

I nodded, feeling a little uneasy at her surprise.

Straightening myself, I tried to give a little more confidence to my answer.

"Yes, Kara Heston. She is still a patient here, correct? This is where the payments go each month."

"No! I mean, yes! She is! She just hasn't had a visitor in such a long time. Years in fact. I'm so happy someone has come to see her. Let me just get the doctor, I'm sure she is going to be thrilled to bring you back to Kara."

While the receptionist scurried away, I looked around the front office. There were pictures of patients, all on the younger side, at least younger than me. In fact, I didn't see one picture in there of anyone any older than me. Which must have meant that this institution, this place, was only for younger people. Most likely under eighteen.

We had turned eighteen last October; in a few days, we'd turn nineteen.

What was going to happen to Kara then?

Clicking of heels in the hall told me that someone was coming fast and furious in my direction. I turned quickly and saw a no-nonsense woman striding towards me. Her white coat floated behind her, blonde, turning white, hair in a tight bun on the top of her head.

She stuck her hand out. Her skin was papery, and her hand was bony, but her shake was strong and sure.

"I'm Dr. Pratt. Are you here to pick up Kara?"

"I...pick up? No. I mean, I didn't even know that Kara was here..." My words trailed off as I tried to find a way to explain the things I didn't even understand.

The smiling receptionist was hovering behind Dr. Pratt and I couldn't sort my thoughts that were flying through my mind. The blackness of my headaches started to cloud my mind.

"Is there someplace we can talk?" I asked.

She nodded and led me back to her office. She didn't say anything more until I was seated, and the door was shut behind us.

"So, if you're not here to pick Kara up, may I ask why you did come? She hasn't had a visitor in years. She's our only patient that never gets to see anyone."

Her voice was soft and smooth, and while she clearly demanded the respect of the room, she had a calming way about her. If she had been Kara's doctor all of these years, I had hoped that whatever had been wrong with her, Dr. Pratt had been able to fix.

"I'm her sister but I didn't know about Kara. I just found out that she even existed," I said.

"Did you think she had passed away?" Dr. Pratt asked in earnest.

I shook my head. I still wasn't explaining myself correctly.

"My mother, she just passed away a few days ago. And she left me this box. And in it was a note explaining about Kara and bringing her here. Along with all of the billing statements, pictures, and her birth certificate. So, it wasn't that I thought she was dead. It was that I never even knew she was born."

Dr. Pratt, who had been leaning on her desk, slid down to sit in the chair next to me.

"Your parents never told you about her? You never spoke about her?"

I shook my head.

"My father has been gone for as long as I can remember. He left us. And my mother...she drank a lot and was more concerned with being social than with me. She died just a few days ago."

An image flashed quickly through my mind. Crushed pills. An open bottle of wine. Particles floating, dissolving...

Her hand fluttered to mind offering my comfort, but I pulled my hand away. I needed to stay focused. I needed to find my sister.

"When I found out that I had a sister, I had to come to see her. I had to find out what had happened, why she was here. And see if we could maybe...I don't know...get to know each other I guess."

"You don't remember her at all?"

I shook my head. I didn't know how to explain it either, how could I forget I had a sister? Let alone a twin. It didn't make sense. I was sure it sounded like I was lying.

"I get headaches a lot...they cause blackouts. I have to take medication for them but sometimes it messes with my memory." It was as much as I was willing to say so that she didn't think I was crazy too. Even with the excuse of the headaches and the medication, it still didn't explain losing the memory of an entire person.

Dr. Pratt didn't say anything but moved slowly to the window behind her desk and stared for a moment. She blew out a breath before she spoke again.

"Do you know much about Holden Lake Institute?" she asked.

"Not really. I didn't look into it much last night," I admitted.

"Of course, of course. You're just learning about all of this." She sat down and opened a file on her desk.

"Holden Lake Institute is for children who are deemed psychologically insane. Sometimes by the courts, sometimes for other reasons. They stay here, go to school here, get therapies here, and once they turn eighteen and graduate from our program, they are able to be released back to their families for supervised outpatient therapy. Or, they are referred to an institution fit for adults."

I listened to what Dr. Pratt was saying and put the pieces together quickly.

"You thought I was here to pick her up, which means you think she is ready to come home?"

Dr. Pratt nodded. "I'd been calling your mother for months to make arrangements for her to come home. But it was to no avail. She never answered or returned my calls. It wasn't completely unexpected, since she nor your father had been to see Kara since she was a young girl. The most recent messages were to inform her that she needed to be picked up and arrangements made, or she was going to be sent somewhere else. The decision needed to be made before her next birthday which would age her out of the program completely."

If my mind wasn't spinning before, it had become like the tilt-a-whirl at the carnival.

"You're looking pale. Do you need some water? Or maybe put your head between your legs and just breathe for a moment."

I waved her off. "No, I'll be fine. This is just a lot to take in."

Dr. Pratt gave me a moment to breathe before she continued. "At this point, we're out of time. Her...well...your birthday is in a few days. You'll have to take her home with you, or we'll be making arrangements to transfer her."

The warmth I had detected in her before was replaced with a stone-like business attitude and suddenly I was missing Mr. O'Neal's pity.

"I'm so sorry to have to do this to you, but you have to make the choice now for her. She will either need to have arrangements made to go home with you, or she moves on to the next institute."

I swallowed. I may have been practically nineteen, but I was not ready to make such a heavy decision about someone I had just learned existed less than twenty-four hours before.

"May I...can I...meet my sister now?"

Chapter 5

As we walked out to a lush green courtyard, I saw that the place really was beautiful. Exactly the type of place you'd want to send someone...if you absolutely had to. Though I still wasn't sure if Kara had ever really needed to be there. Or if my parents just hadn't known what else to do.

Dr. Pratt spoke as we walked. "Your sister has been a model patient for years. I said that in messages to your mother. I even told her that she was most likely able to come back home years ago when she was still a child...but your mother insisted."

She led me to a set of outdoor chairs and tables, and I grabbed hold of one to brace myself. Had she just said what I thought she did?

"Do you mean that all this time my sister didn't need to be here?"

Dr. Pratt gestured to the chair for me to take a seat. I hesitated but saw that she wasn't going to answer my question until I was seated. There was a level of control that Dr. Pratt demanded. Some part of me wanted to defy that, to push the chair at her, to fight that know-it-all attitude. I held out for a few moments before I decided I wanted the answer more than I wanted to fight with her. But something inside of me was still bubbling hot, a lot like the feeling I had had inside of Mr. O'Neal's office.

"When she first got here, I would say she needed to be here. She was aggressive, fighting with staff every step of the way. Insisting that she didn't need to be here, that nothing was wrong with her. That she'd done nothing wrong. She would scream and yell about it all day and night. Now, she was quite young at the time, not even five, so tantrums were to be expected. Especially after what your parents had told us about her...aggressions. But eventually, she got in line like they always do. The screaming and yelling subsided and finally, she made peace that she needed to get well. I can't say we've had any concerns or problems for years."

If that was true, then why hadn't she come home? Why hadn't my mother gone there to get her, to make us a family? If losing Kara was what had driven my father away and what had turned my mother into a cold drunk, then why hadn't they wanted to bring her home? To reverse the sands of time?

I stood quietly for a few moments, wondering how life may have been different if things with Kara had been different. Would my father have come home? Would my mother have stopped drinking and bonded with her daughters? Would I have had a real family?

Voices floated from the other side of the courtyard and it snapped me from my questions. Turning towards the sound of conversation I looked and saw a nurse walking and talking with...me.

Her hair wasn't cut as smoothly as mine, and it hadn't been conditioned as nicely either.

Her walk was a bit stiffer than mine. I wondered what type of physical exercise she got in the institution versus what I was able to get outside of it. I was given ballet lessons, tennis lessons, and any other lessons I'd wanted. What had Kara been able to learn?

Her face had no makeup, except for a slight pink tint to her lips; a lip balm probably. Versus myself who had top-of-the-line makeup and routine facials.

And of course, her clothes were those of the institution, all the way down to her slip-on shoes. Whereas I couldn't remember which boutique I'd even gotten my outfit from, or how much I'd charged on my credit card for it.

But at the heart of it all...despite the differences that life had caused...my mother had been right. We were practically impossible to tell apart.

I scanned her face, looking for a fleck of different color in her eyes or even a freckle that might give the distinction between us.

There was none.

We were exactly alike.

My sister and I stared at each other, examining each other, seeing our own confused reflection mirrored back to us.

Dr. Pratt looked pleased as she stood between us. "Why don't we give these two some time to catch up? I'm sure they have lots to talk about."

The nurse and Dr. Pratt walked towards the main building and took a seat on a bench outside of it. Far enough away to give us some privacy, close enough to intervene if something went wrong.

"So, you're...my sister," I said. It was a horrible first opening line but nothing else came to my mind.

Kara nodded, strands of her hair falling slightly in front of her face to brush her cheek.

She twitched her head in the direction of the nurse. "Betty over there told me that you didn't know I was here," she said.

God, even the way she spoke was exactly the same. The tone, the cadence, the words. It took everything I had to not reach out and touch her to make sure this wasn't some wild dream or hallucination. The pills had caused that to happen before, not often, but for a second it did make me question. Somehow though, I knew this was real.

"I didn't know you even existed. I was given a letter from Mom, explaining everything. She died a few days ago and she left me the bank account and information."

Kara's eyes went wide. "Mom died?"

For some reason, I would have expected they would have told her that. My stomach twisted when I realized the callous way I had blurted out the information. I may not have been close with my mother, but maybe Kara had loved her. After all, she didn't have to live with the showy lush that I did. Then again, she was the same mother that had dumped her in an institution and left her there to rot.

"I'm sorry, I thought they would have told you. Yes, they believed she overdosed on a mix of pills and booze." I tried to find compassion in my voice but if it had been hard to have it before, it was even more impossible now that I knew she had been keeping my own twin sister from me.

"She killed herself?"

I shrugged. Suicide? Accident? The truth was...well...no one really knew the truth.

Kara stared off into the courtyard, what she was seeing I didn't know. A small smile ghosted across her lips. Like she knew something she didn't want to say.

I changed the topic back to what Dr. Pratt wanted from me.

"They told me that they had been trying to contact Mom because you're ready to come home."

"They tell me that I've been ready for a long time. But Mom stopped answering them. She kept paying, every month right on time, but she never answered. Now that I...we're...going to be nineteen...I thought I'd get to come home. I didn't think she would ignore me until they sent me somewhere else."

While my sister stared off into the distance, lost in her own thoughts, I knew there was only one thing to do.

"Do you want to come home? Do you want to come live with me?"

Slowly, she turned to look at me. Her eyes stared straight into mine.

"You'd be okay with that?"

A breeze blew past us, rustling both of our loose hair, but I got a chill when it happened while Kara stayed perfectly still.

"Well, it's either that or you have to go to another institute, one that probably isn't as nice as this one. Your doctor says you're ready to come home. And neither one of us has any family left. It's just us."

I didn't know what I expected. A smile maybe. A slight relaxation to her tense, squared shoulders. But there was no reaction from her at all. Not for a few moments while she continued to stare at me, almost like she was staring into me.

"I don't think there's any other option," she said.

Footsteps padded on the grass behind us and I turned to see Dr. Pratt and Nurse Betty walking up to us.

"How is it going here?" Dr. Pratt asked.

I paused, wondering who was going to be the one who answered.

In the end, it was me. "I think we've made a decision."

Chapter 6

They only gave me one day to get things settled at home and get back to bring Kara home with me. With our birthday being in just a couple of days, she couldn't stay any longer.

Dr. Pratt got right to work, setting up a schedule for Kara, benchmarks she was going to have to hit such as going to school or finding a job, and outpatient therapies she was required to attend. She was even given a nightly curfew to make sure she wasn't out getting in any trouble. There would be an assigned caseworker and if any missteps took place, there would be consequences. She would be placed in a halfway house or back in an institution.

Kara was going to need to prove that she could succeed in society.

I was almost jealous that she was the one coming out of the institution. If I had been there maybe I would have had a better outlook for my own life. At the moment, I had no idea if I was going to get a full-time job, go to school full-time, a bit of both, go to trade school...there were so many options. When I graduated high school, my mother didn't care what I did so I did nothing. Kara was lucky that she had people that were going to help her through figuring it all out.

There wasn't time for me to decide if I was even ready for a sister. Especially one that would take the kind of care she would need. But it was the last chance I had to have a family and I was not going to be the one who continued to let Kara rot away.

My hands shook as I spilled out a pill and popped it in my mouth, swallowing it dry. The headaches had been pressing worse lately and I didn't want the black pain to ruin the day. I made a mental note that I was going to have to get a refill soon, the bottle was more empty than I had realized.

With a deep breath and no idea what I was doing, I got out of the car and walked across the parking lot.

Dr. Pratt had been waiting with Kara at the door with her bags. It was like they couldn't get her out fast enough.

"We just have a few things for you to sign and you girls can be on your way," she said.

The papers seemed standard, though I was wondering if I should have brought Mr. O'Neal along with me to help me understand the legal wording. From the gist of it all, I gathered that Kara was going to be my responsibility. While she was going to have her caseworker and every other resource they were giving her, ultimately it was going to be on my shoulders to make sure she succeeded in it all.

Once my last signature was on the paperwork, Dr. Pratt showed us to the front door. I wondered what was going through Kara's mind as she took her first true free steps from that place. It hadn't seemed like a horrible place to grow up in, but it wasn't the same as being free.

I wanted to ask her what she was thinking, what she was feeling; if she was as nervous or as excited as I was.

I had always thought that twins were able to read each other's minds or feel the same things without even saying a word. But on the drive home, I didn't feel any kind of connection like that. Maybe it would come in time after we got to know each other again, or maybe it was just a connection we never had.

Instead, the drive was peppered with small talk until we neared home.

"Do you want to order a pizza or something? We can have it delivered so by the time you've unpacked it'll be ready," I offered.

"Pizza...wow...like fresh pizza?" There was an awe in her voice that gave me a pang of something strange.

What would it have been like to be stuck in there for so long that fresh pizza seemed like a treat?

"We'll get double cheese," I offered clearly trying to find a way to ease some of my guilt.

Her few items were already unpacked in the spare room by the time the doorbell rang, and the pizza guy was there.

In the kitchen, I took out some paper plates and lifted a couple of slices from the box.

"That used to be my room," she said.

I jumped, startled to feel that she was right behind me. Whirling around, I saw her waiting, expectantly. I handed her the pizza but that wasn't what she was waiting for.

"The spare room...it used to be yours?"

"Where did you think I slept?"

"I guess I thought you slept in my room. I mean, we were young. It would have made sense for us to share a room."

Kara took a bite of pizza and the cheese strung long as she tried to cut it with her teeth.

"This is so good, wow. I haven't had real food in a long time," she said through a mouthful.

I took my plate and walked over to the kitchen table. I tried to picture our little family of four sitting around the table eating together, but my mind drew a blank. I remembered the table...I even remembered my father a little. But Kara was nowhere in my memory banks.

"Do you remember a lot? About this house or our family?" I suddenly blurted.

Kara swallowed and froze, just as she did outside in the courtyard, her eyes like steel. I got another chill, but it wasn't from any kind of breeze.

"I remember everything."

The rest of the night went about just as stiffly. Just as awkwardly.

I didn't truly have many expectations for what it was going to be like living with Kara, but it didn't seem to be going well.

Though any start was a start.

The clock blinked three in the morning when I stirred from my sleep, a nightmare lingering in the corner of my mind.

I blinked in the darkness, trying to erase the images. A screeching cat, dark tar pouring from a gash in its neck, laughter floating above it all...

A shadow moved across the doorframe.

My heart bursting with fear, I sprang up and knocked everything off my nightstand as I tried to find the table light.

Kara was standing in the doorframe, rocking gently from foot to foot.

"Shit Kara, you scared the hell out of me! Is everything okay? Is something wrong?"

She was silent for so long, I wondered if she even heard me.

"I was wrong. This was my room."

She stood and stared at me for a moment longer before she shuffled slowly back to bed.

I didn't say a word. I had no idea what to say because I didn't have any idea what the hell had just happened.

Was she sleepwalking? Did she do that? Wouldn't they have wanted to warn me of something like that?

I didn't sleep the rest of the night.

Chapter 7

"Was everything okay last night?" I asked while I poured two bowls of cereal the next morning.

She took a bowl and grabbed two silver spoons from the utensil drawer. I realized I hadn't shown her where they were since the night before we had eaten pizza and hadn't needed the silverware.

Kara really did remember everything.

"Yeah, things were fine. I slept well. You?"

I took my bowl off of the kitchen counter and accepted the spoon she handed me. We both moved over to the kitchen table in perfect unison.

"I guess I slept okay," I hedged. There was no way I had dreamt what had happened the night before. "But you did come into my room last night. Were you sleepwalking or something?"

She crunched her cinnamon squares. "No, I don't sleepwalk."

"Are you upset that I'm in your room then? I don't remember having my room moved when I was little, but I guess I don't remember much from back then."

"You didn't need to remember like I did. You were still living it. I was the one who needed to play the memories in my mind." Kara's eyes met mine. "If I had forgotten everything, I may not even know who I really am anymore."

"I'm sorry," I said, the guilt heavy in my words. It wasn't my fault that our parents had put her there, but it was my fault that I didn't remember her. "Do you want your room back? We can put your stuff in there and then decorate it how you want. I can move my stuff to the other room. It's no problem."

Her eyes were still set on mine. "You can't fix things that easily. It doesn't work like that."

The rest of the breakfast was eaten in silence.

I needed to try again with her, to find a way to form that twin connection. Things weren't right between us and I knew it was my responsibility to make it right. I was the one who had gotten to live a normal life. She was the one who had never been able to have a childhood or have any part of a regular life.

While I cleaned up the breakfast dishes, she sat and stared out the window.

What memories was she replaying? What did she see that I couldn't see?

"Did you want to do something today? Maybe go to the mall or.... well...I'm not really sure what it is you like to do."

"Neither am I," she said and continued to stare out the window. "But no. I used one of those apps on your phone to get a car here. I have to go get some things done today, things my caseworker wants me to do before I meet with her next week."

I looked down at my phone, wondering when I had even left it alone for her to go into it. It didn't matter though, what was mine was hers. Still, it felt a little strange.

"You should have told me. I'd have taken you anywhere you needed to go."

She shook her head, her eyes finally moving from the window as if she was remembering she was inside rather than out wherever she thought she was.

"I'd rather go alone. It's time I do things on my own. I need to be on my own."

I sat back down across from her and searched her face. I was trying to reach her, to try and make a connection, but it was as if she was intentionally putting up a wall against us. She was blocking me out. It was like she was angry at me for the fact that she had been sent there.

Or maybe she was mad because I didn't know she had even existed. If it had been me locked away, never even giving anyone a problem in all my years there, and my family acted as if I didn't exist...I probably would have been angry at everyone too.

But I didn't know how to make it up to her, I couldn't change the past.

I put my hand on her arm and she jumped. Goosebumps rose on her arm under where I touched her, and I quickly recoiled.

"I'm sorry Kara, I really am sorry. I don't know why you were sent there, and I know I'll never truly know everything that happened or why our parents acted as if you weren't born, but I want to make it up to you. You're all I've got. And I want to make things right. I can't erase the past, but I want us to have a future as sisters."

Suddenly, she shoved back from the table and stood up so quickly that the chair rocked back and almost tipped over.

"You think just one apology makes up for it? Do you actually think one apology, where you admit you have no idea what happened and why, when you got to live this cushy life while I was locked away, makes up for everything? You can't just tell me you're sorry and declare that you want a sister and poof I become one."

Her face was turning red, the same look that I would get on my face when I was pissed, and her body was shaking. How could she be so angry at me- what had I ever done to her? Other than forgetting her.

"Do you blame me for all of this? Do you think somehow this is my fault?"

Tires crunched on the loose stone outside and we both turned to see that her car was pulling into the driveway.

The red in her face drained and her shaking stopped...a storm that had been threatening to tear the place apart had just subsided. And I had no real idea of what had caused it.

Kara flashed a quick smile before she took a small, frayed purse and slung it over her shoulder.

"Not sure when I'll be back. I'll see you later," she said. It was as if nothing had happened at all.

Chapter 8

I didn't hear from Kara for the rest of the day.

In the first few hours, it didn't seem like such a big deal. She said she had some things to do and she was out and had freedom for the very first time in her life. If I was in her shoes I would want to get out and be alone too.

But by the time it started to get dark, and closer to her curfew, I began to worry.

Should I have insisted I go with her? She didn't have a phone, she didn't know her way around, she didn't even know how the world worked. And she was out there in it alone.

I had made some dinner for us, nothing fancy since cooking wasn't my strongest attribute, but still, I had tried. I seemed to be the only person out of the two of us who was trying to have any kind of relationship. I understood that she was upset but the longer she stayed out, the more frustrated I became.

Her grilled cheese went cold and her soup got a film, both of which I tossed before I started pacing the house waiting for her. If she didn't show up, was I supposed to call someone? Her caseworker? Her doctor?

Was she hurt? Did she run away?

Had she hurt someone else?

I hated myself for that last thought. Dr. Pratt said she hadn't caused any problems in the years since she'd settled into Holden Lake. But still, the thought had popped into my mind.

My parents hadn't just sent her away for no reason, there had to be a real reason. And what was with that thing last night, standing at my door and watching me sleep?

It was creepy.

My thoughts began to swirl faster and more furious until I popped one of my pills to calm it down. It was thirty minutes before her curfew when I heard the stones crunch again.

All the tension fell away when I knew she was back home and was safe.

"Hey!" I said it even too brightly for me. "How did everything go today?"

Kara shrugged like a sullen teenager and put some shopping bags on the table. I hated that I was acting like some hovering parent but technically, I had signed the papers that she was my responsibility.

"It was fine. I got a phone and got some things set up for my future."

"Wow...future. Seems like a big word. I haven't even thought about mine."

She was rifling through a bigger purse, a newer one. "I haven't stopped thinking about my future for years. All I could think about was what I would do when I was finally out."

An awkward silence settled in the room between us.

"So, what did you get?" I asked trying to change gears. It seemed every time we spoke, she was angry, bringing up the past, a past I couldn't change.

"Part of Mom's payments to the institute was into an account. For expenses that I needed there and what I would need when I got out just in case no one came to claim me. So, I took some of that money and went shopping. Some clothes that aren't from donations to Holden, a new purse, a phone...stuff like that."

I nodded as she pulled items out of the bags to show me. "Seems like it was a fun day," I said. There was a sting inside of me that I kind of wished she had asked me to go along. A shopping day seemed like a good way to bond.

"Yeah, I think I've gotten most of what I need to get started."

"Started in what?" I asked.

A tiny giggle escaped her. "My new life of course. Just a few more things and I'll know I'm truly free."

"You don't feel free now?" I asked.

"Not quite yet," she said her voice low and distant. "But I will be soon."

"Is...is there anything...can I help?"

Kara walked towards me and put a cool hand on my cheek. It was my turn to jump.

"Oh Sister, you've helped more than enough." With her bags, she brushed past me and to the stairs.

"Are you going to bed already? We haven't had any time to hang out today and talk," I said.

"You'll be seeing me. Goodnight," she said in a singsong voice.

I watched her go up the stairs, yet another person in my life that didn't want me there.

That night, the dreams were more real than ever.

Screaming, constant wailing rang through them all night long.

There was an apple tree, with a horrifying face in the shadows of its bark. From the space where the eyes would be, blood started to seep. Then from its nose. Then it began to pour like a fountain from its mouth. Blood seeped into the ground, turning the grass into a lake of crimson blood.

I woke with a start, my body sticky with sweat.

My head was hurting worse than usual. Pressure building behind my eyes. I stretched my sore muscles that had been locked tensely during the nightmare. With a sigh, I rolled over to reach for my pills and my hand landed in something wet on my sheet.

Had I knocked over my water cup from my nightstand in my nightmare fit?

I blinked my eyes open but couldn't make out anything in the dark room. As my senses came back to me and out of the dream, the wet spot didn't feel like water. It felt...thicker.

What was that?

Sitting up, I clicked on the lamp on the nightstand.

It took a long moment for my mind to believe what my eyes were seeing.

It was a bird. A dead bird. Laying in my sheets. Blood pooled underneath its wings.

A scream ripped out of me.

Kara clicked on the light in my bedroom within a second. "Problem?" she asked, with very little concern in her voice.

"There's a dead damn bird in the bed! How the hell did it get here? Did you put it here?" I screamed at her.

I scrambled from the bed and pushed past her to get to the bathroom where I scrubbed my hands of the blood.

"Why would I do that Sister?" she asked.

"I don't know! Why *would* you do something like that? It's disgusting!"

Kara appeared in the mirror behind me. "I didn't put it in your bed. Maybe the cat did," she said.

I whirled around to stare at her. "Cat? The cat did it? I don't have a cat! I've never been able to have a pet in my life!"

"Hm...don't you think that's strange? Not even a hamster or something? Why weren't you able to have a pet?"

"I...I don't know...Mom was allergic or something," I said rather confused by the change in questioning. A shadow of a memory slipped into my mind. Something in the note my mother wrote...

"It doesn't matter why I couldn't have a cat. The point is I don't have a cat so why the hell did you put a bird in my bed like that?"

Just then, a cat ran screeching from Kara's bedroom, darted through the hall, and down the stairs.

"Was that a cat?" I screamed.

"You should lower your voice before the neighbors think there is a problem. I'm sure they wouldn't be too happy to know you've brought me home."

My voice had still been frantic and tense whereas Kara's voice was low and steady.

I snapped my mouth shut. What was she talking about? Why wouldn't they want her home with me? And that was a good question.... what did the neighbors think about my sister being shipped away all those years ago? Why had they never brought her up? Then again, how many times had I ever seen our neighbors even speak to us?

My head was starting to throb. I was going to need some of my pills in a minute, but I had to figure out what was happening in my own house. The pills always made me foggy and confused.

"I thought that was your cat. It was at the backdoor meowing, so I let it in the other night when I was awake. I thought it was one of those indoor, outdoor cats. I guess I was wrong," she said simply. "I'm going back to bed. I have things to do in the morning."

I tried to shake my mind loose of the thoughts that were jamming together.

"How did you get to my room so fast? Were you standing outside of it again?"

"It's my room," she said and walked back to bed.

Chapter 9

There was no more sleep for me that night. How could I sleep when my sister was...well...I didn't know exactly what she was.

Creepy was the only word that popped into my head and I immediately felt bad for the thought.

She had lived in an institution, abandoned by her own family for most of her life. Of course, she was going to be a little...off.

But something inside of me was telling me it was something else. That there was some other reason that she was acting so weird.

The next morning, she was gone before I even got out of bed. I heard her rustling around downstairs and part of me wanted to go and help her get some breakfast and eat with her. But I couldn't leave my bed. I was actually terrified to go downstairs. I didn't want to have a run-in with her. I didn't want to have to talk to her or see her.

Maybe I had been better off alone. Maybe I never should have brought her home with me.

Dr. Pratt had insisted that she was healthy and that there was no reason for her to have to move to another institution. If I couldn't trust the opinion of a doctor, then who could I trust?

Aunt Cheryl.

Surely, she would know what had happened all the way back then, why my parents had thought to lock Kara up. Why my mother had told me to never let her out. My mother was a lot of things but she couldn't have been that cruel to let a sane girl stay institutionalized. There had to be some sense to this somewhere. Maybe if I just understood the reason then that would help me get some clarity.

It was possible that I was being paranoid. Kara's life had flipped upside down just like mine had. There was bound to be an adjustment period. Still, I was desperate for answers. Aunt Cheryl didn't answer when I called. So, I left a message and waited.

I tried to go about my day but the longer I waited to hear from her, the more anxious I became.

On my own, I tried to search my memory, to try to find some rationalization. But my mind kept coming up empty. I couldn't remember a thing and without a memory of back then, I couldn't fathom my parent's reasons. Sure, they hadn't been great parents, but I didn't think they would have just dumped one of us off and kept the other.

I tried Aunt Cheryl again.

And again.

And again.

I paced my house, unable to settle down, alternating between telling myself I was being ridiculous and telling myself that it was completely logical to be worried since I really didn't know Kara's history and she was so strange.

As the clock got closer to Kara's curfew, the worry that she wouldn't make it back on time started to weigh on me as well.

Instead of being worried about the story behind Kara, I started being worried about where she was and what she was doing.

And then the guilt hit.

I should have been worried about her the whole time instead of worried about her past.

Just like a watched pot never boils, the moment I stopped wondering about Kara was when my phone rang. I answered it without even looking at the screen, I knew it was only going to be one person.

She didn't even say hello.

"Don't tell me you let Kara out of the institute."

"I...well...yea, I brought her home with me," I stuttered back. "They told me that she was fine, that she hadn't had any episodes in years. And if I didn't take her with me then they were going to send her to another institute." The more I explained the more bravado I felt. I had done the right thing; I knew I had. No matter what my mother's instructions had been.

At least that's what I was telling myself.

"No, no she has to go back. She needs to be locked away; this was a mistake. A huge mistake. Damn, I wish I had gotten your call before. I had no idea they would ever let you take her out of there."

Aunt Cheryl was rambling but the more she did the more intense her words grew.

"I don't understand. Dr. Pratt said she was fine to come home."

"Oh, I'm sure she did. Your sister...she was always good at manipulating people. But make no mistake about it, that girl is dangerous. I suggest you call the police right now and have her taken away."

"What? Why would I do that? That's crazy! She hasn't done anything wrong."

"How did you know about her? Your mother didn't want..."

"She left me a letter. And a box. It told me to keep paying but I couldn't do that. Not when I went there to see her. Not after speaking to her doctor. She had aged out of the program. They were going to send her somewhere else. I couldn't let that happen, she's my sister."

"Kylie, listen to me, your sister isn't right. Heaven help me I always told your mother it was something about being born at midnight on Halloween, but she never listened to me. Your sister, she was evil right from the start. Didn't your mom's letter tell you anything?"

"It said that she was aggressive, a bit harmful and my parents were worried. But Dr. Pratt said..."

"It doesn't matter what Dr. Pratt said. Dr. Pratt was a part of the cover-up to begin with. Your parents paid a great deal of money to that place and Dr. Pratt took on the challenge to fix her. But there was no fixing her, not after what she had done."

I wasn't sure I wanted to know anymore what Kara had done. Part of me wanted to hang up and just try and find a new way to bond with my sister. I hadn't seen Aunt Cheryl in years, what did she even know? Still...I needed to know the real reason Kara was locked away.

I could hear her take a deep, steadying breath on the other end.

"One day, a boy named Nigel from down the street went missing. You were so young; I don't believe you would remember any of this. He was a little older than you and your sister, maybe a year or two. He didn't come home from playing and his parents were frantic. They formed a search party and we all went up and down the street calling his name.

We found him. Under an apple tree. Blood was drying from a wound on his head. He was dead.

It was ruled an accident. They said he must have hit his head on a nearby rock when he fell from climbing the tree.

But your sister...she had come home that night with blood on her clothes.

It was no accident.

Your parents couldn't admit what she'd done, they couldn't accept it. So, they paid to make it go away. They paid for her to be put in an institution and to keep her there where a young doctor was eager to take the challenge to cure her. The neighborhood was so distraught over Nigel that they didn't think much of it when they told them she was having developmental issues and was being sent to a school that could help her.

Your sister is a murderer.

It destroyed your family. It destroyed your mother. She couldn't believe she had brought that monster into the world and I couldn't forgive her for not telling Nigel's mother the truth. And the police.

Your father blamed his leaving on the fact that your mother couldn't move on, but he was never the same once they dropped her off."

Ice-cold terror streaked through my blood.

The nightmares. They all made sense. They weren't just dreams, but pictures of my memory.

"Did you get the answers you were looking for Sister?" Kara's voice behind me made me jump, and my phone clattered to the floor.

Chapter 10

"Kara...I...I mean...you're kind of late, aren't you?" I asked, trying to buy some time,

I stood from the couch and tried to remain calm while my mind was racing.

"I made curfew though, didn't I?" She tilted her head the same way I did when I was feigning innocence.

I knew now that she was far from innocent.

"Yes, you did. I just thought you would have been here earlier. We didn't even get to hang out today." It was an attempt to sound light and calm, but I knew I wasn't fooling anyone.

With each step I took backward, away from Kara, she mirrored my steps forward.

"It doesn't seem like you needed to spend time with me, it sounds like Aunt Cheryl already filled you in on our little family history." Kara's grin stretched wide and maniacal.

I shuddered.

"I don't know if I even believe what she said. I have barely spoken to the woman in years...I have no problem just forgetting everything."

Kara's hand moved subtly from behind her back and I saw the glint of a large kitchen knife.

My heart leaped into my throat as my mouth went dry.

"That's the problem though isn't it, Sister? You can't forget. Can you?" It was a question that wasn't a question. "Just because you didn't remember me, doesn't mean I didn't remember you. I remembered everything. And from the crying I could hear from your room at night, I know you remember too."

My eyes darted around the room, searching for a way out. Kara was blocking the only exit and I was a cornered animal, caught and waiting for its death.

I was certain that's what she was going for.

"See the thing is though, they got it all wrong. I didn't murder Nigel, I didn't hurt those kids, I didn't kill those animals. It was all a misunderstanding."

My mind was looking for a way out.

"A misunderstanding?" Maybe if I could talk her down, and keep her distracted, then I could find a way out.

"Of course. Because I didn't do any of that. I knew it all along." Kara's voice was calm, serene almost, and she took a seat on the edge of the couch. "See, I knew it when I went in there, that I hadn't done anything. I didn't understand why Mom and Dad had just dropped me off and left me there. As you can imagine it was quite traumatic."

Her eyes were trained on the blade and I wished I could understand what she was thinking. I wished like hell we had that twin vibe. But I had nothing, no idea what she was going to say or do.

"I fought them, the doctors, everyone, all the way. I kept telling them I didn't belong there. But it didn't matter, they didn't want to hear it. And eventually, I realized the only way to get out was to play along. To take my medications and do the therapy and act as if I was getting better."

"But you weren't?" I asked, now becoming more interested in her story and less worried about getting out of the room. Maybe all she really needed was for someone to finally listen to her.

"There was nothing for me to get better from. I wasn't the one who was sick. No one would listen to me though, they all thought I was crazy. Do you know some people actually blamed my birthday being on Halloween? Isn't *that* crazy?"

Aunt Cheryl had done the same thing, but I wasn't going to tell her that. I needed to keep her talking. The more she talked, the calmer she seemed to be. And the calmer she was, the less tightly I saw she was holding onto that knife.

When I didn't answer, she looked up and met my eyes in that chilling way she had.

"I guess it wasn't really so crazy. Maybe Halloween did have a little something to do with it. Except here's the catch....my birthday isn't on Halloween. Yours is."

"What? No, my birthday is the day before Halloween. Yours is Halloween."

Kara stood from the couch and slowly started taking steps towards me, the grip on the knife tight again.

"See, that's what they all kept telling me too. In therapy. They kept telling me that my reality was distorted. That I was trying to change my past to cover what I did. But I knew...I was certain...that I knew who I was and what I had done. And what I hadn't done. Since no one would listen, I knew I'd have to prove it. So, one day, I paid someone off with the money that Mom would send me, and I did a kit that I found online. It matches DNA with fingerprints to find a birth certificate. And do you know what I found out?"

I shook my head, not sure that I even wanted to hear anymore.

"Oh, come on, tell me you want to know," she said with a wild giggle.

I shook my head again, unable to speak.

"Tell me!" Her giggles turned to shouting as she thrust the knife toward me.

"I want to know! Tell me!" I cried.

"Oh, it's just too good," she took another step forward and I took a giant step back, pinning my back to the wall.

I was trapped.

"I learned they got the wrong twin."

My stomach sank.

"Have you noticed we don't even have a freckle of a difference between us? Apparently, that can cause some confusion with teachers, neighbors, and even your parents when a little boy has been killed. I didn't do any of those things sister. Was I there? Yes. But was I the monster? No sister, that was you."

Flashes of my nightmares blinded my mind, and I closed my eyes to try and shake away the thoughts.

"No...no that isn't possible! I would remember. I would remember doing those things. I haven't done anything to hurt anybody, ever!"

"Are you sure about that? Can you really remember it all? Because up until a few days ago, you didn't even remember you had a twin. But the truth is, you do. So, Sister, what other truths are you hiding from yourself? Your nightmares should have told you. Or do you need another pill? That should help you keep blocking things out. Maybe you don't have enough left...I suppose it depends on how many you slipped in Mother's drink."

My eyes went wide, and she mirrored me, mocking my shock on her own face.

"Shhh...don't worry. I won't tell anyone."

Dizziness took over as the images grew louder in my mind.

No. None of this could be true. It was all lies. It had to be. I'd remember killing someone. I'd remember hurting someone. I'd never done anything wrong to anyone.

But those headaches, those blackouts, the horrible images I couldn't explain...

Kara began to laugh, the most evil sound I'd ever heard. "Putting the pieces together? Finally. It's amazing you could hide from yourself as well as you did for so long."

"No, no, no," I kept chanting as if I kept saying them then I could erase it all. "This is all a lie. You're lying to me!" I screamed.

Searing pain shot through my abdomen.

I looked into Kara's eyes as she twisted the knife deeper inside of me.

"Why?" I burbled through the blood coming from my lips.

"You took my life while you got one of your own. You erased it all while I lived with your consequences. I wasn't the killer...but...I suppose I am now."

She ripped the knife from my stomach, and I dropped to the floor.

My sister looked down at me as I bled out onto the carpet. I reached my hand up to hers, begging for help without any words.

A clock in the house rang out. It was midnight. I hadn't even realized what the day was. But suddenly, it hit me.

Kara gave me one last look and a smile that curled my insides.

"Happy Halloween Sister. Oh, and happy birthday."

Chapter 11

DANGEROUS MENTAL PATIENT ESCAPED

Kara Heston, a recently released mental patient, has run away from her home. Kara, now nineteen years old, was released into her sister's care just days before. Her twin sister, Kylie, was stabbed and left to die before the patient fled. If not for a well-check called by the victim's aunt, Kylie surely would have died.

She remains in critical condition.

If anyone has any information about Kara Heston, please make no attempts to speak to her. Call local authorities immediately. She is considered extremely dangerous.

I read the article.

Who is really the dangerous one?

I'll never know the answer to that question. No one will. What were lies? What was the truth? Who is Kara? Who am I?

If she is right, I am the killer. And I should have been the one locked away.

Of course, she could have been wrong, she could just be crazy. But I've had enough time in the hospital recovering to think about it all. I don't think she was wrong.

Well...except...she was wrong about one thing.

She isn't a killer. I'm not dead.

But now I know who I really am. It's time I stop hiding.

I don't think I'm going to take those headache pills anymore.

Happy Birthday, Sister.

II
DEAR SISTER

Chapter 1

Kylie

"Are you sure that you want to go through with this?"

I stopped twisting the hair tie on my wrist which was making red marks on my skin.

"Is there even a choice," I mumbled the question but it wasn't really a question.

Dr. Patrick and I had been over and over this same conversation for months now. Like a circle, it wasn't going anywhere. Just around and around.

Our therapy sessions had almost become predictably routine and I wasn't getting any better.

"Are you taking your medications?"

"Yes."

"Are you still having the nightmares?"

"Yes."

"Have you heard at all from Kara?"

"No."

It would have at least made the sessions more interesting if we had been playing two truths and a lie.

"This operation you're going to have tomorrow, you know there's no guarantee. Sometimes I'm not even sure I should have told you about it."

I sat quietly, unwilling to hash this out for the hundredth time.

Of course, brain surgery wasn't a guarantee. That's like stating that snow is cold. But what other choice did I have?

I'd become frozen in a place that I had no hope of escaping.

I was stuck in a world where I couldn't remember my past but I also couldn't seem to forget it. The flickers of images were always the same, never coming into focus and never leaving me alone.

Was I taking the easy way out? Probably. But I'd been digging for a year, trying to find the truth of my past.

Who was the real monster? Was it me? Was it my sister?

Was what she said true? Or was it the words of a master manipulator?

Aunt Cheryl had flown home when she found out I'd been in the hospital because of Kara. The guilt she wore was like a heavy coat weighing her down. While she stayed with me as I healed, she would alternate between apologizing for never telling me about Kara and continually insisting that it was indeed Kara who belonged in the institute. She'd sworn that Kara was always good at spinning her lies, that's why it took so long for my parents to see what she was when we were kids. Kara always had an explanation and an innocent face.

The same as mine.

Still, there was a feeling in the pit of my stomach, one that felt like a settled stone, that told me I didn't know the whole story.

That's what therapy had been for. To help me find the repressed memories, to help me understand the truth of my own life. But as much as Dr. Patrick had been trying to get me to remember and deal with my reality, my mind had not let it happen.

A clock ticked on the wall and I knew that time was running out.

"I know there isn't a guarantee but nothing else has worked. I need this surgery. I can't stay in this life."

"We can give it more time. Once you do this, you can't undo it. Your life is going to be changed in every way. Are you really ready for that?"

I breathed in and out, slowly and steadily, letting the rest of the time tick by.

Finally, Dr. Patrick closed his notebook and stood from his overstuffed armchair. That was the signal that my time had come to an end.

This would be the last time he saw me until after my surgery.

I ran my fingers across the soft velvet of the couch. I liked this couch. Its rich fabric- a contrast to its deeply relaxing color.

I hoped I'd remember it when this was all over.

Then again, I hoped I'd remember a lot of things.

Wordlessly he walked to his office door and opened it for me. I took a last look around the room, a place that I'd been going to a few times a week, for almost a year, and still, I had no answers.

The disapproval was heavy between us as I walked past him to leave the room for the last time.

"I hope that it does change everything," I said.

I WAS TOLD NOT TO HAVE food or drink after midnight and to avoid alcohol for forty-eight hours before the surgery.

One little glass wasn't going to kill me.

After all, I was going to literally have someone cut open my skull and stick probs into my hippocampus, where my episodic and long-term memories were supposed to be stored. This was supposed to stimulate the deeply rooted memories about my life that I seemingly had been unable to recall.

If the surgery was successful, I'd be able to finally remember what had happened as a child. I'd be able to remember Kara and the truth of our lives.

However, if the surgery was a failure, it could potentially erase my memory entirely.

This would be one of the first times this surgery was going to be performed as a therapeutic treatment. Dr. Patrick had mentioned it in passing one day when all other options had failed. We had tried medication and therapy sessions, but we had also tried hypnotherapy, sensory stimulation, vitamins, and everything else we could think of. This was the last option.

So, I was either going to wake up in the hospital the next day with traumatizing memories and a truth that I was more scared to learn than I wanted to admit. Or, I wasn't going to even know my own name.

I fully believe that the risk I was taking was worth one little glass of wine.

Taking a sip, I settled onto my couch, which was not nearly as comfortable as Dr. Patrick's couch, and set a thick manila folder on my lap.

There was another reason that I was choosing to indulge in a little liquid courage.

Dr. Patrick *should* have been playing two truths and a lie with me.

Truth- I had been taking my medication.

Truth- The nightmares were still there.

Lie- I had heard from my sister.

I'd been getting letters for a year. There was never a return address. Only mine, small in the corner, and her name scrawled in big letters on the front.

KARA

The first time I saw her name written across a blue envelope, I nearly dropped it right on the pavement under the mailbox.

I knew she was alive, that part wasn't shocking. But why would she be writing to me? What more could she possibly have to say?

I sat at the kitchen table all night long, staring at her handwriting on the envelope. Eventually, I decided that whatever she had to say, I didn't want to know. So, I walked it to the garbage can but instead of opening the lid and dropping it inside, I slid it into a drawer.

Before I knew it, I had a whole drawer full of unopened envelopes, all with her name written across the center.

I never told anyone about the letters.

But if there was ever a time to open them, it would have to be the night before my surgery.

Armed with my glass of wine and the knowledge that the next day, everything would change anyway, I opened the folder where I had hidden the letters. The first letter she sent me was right on top, and each one after was filed behind it in chronological order. From the first thing she wanted to tell me, until the last.

Using a letter opener, I slid the blade through and slashed open the paper.

My hands shook as I reached inside and I pulled out her letter. Unfolding it, I took a deep, steadying breath.

Then, I began to read.

Chapter 2

Dear Sister,

By now, you must have many questions.

You want to know the truth- which one of us should have been locked away. Do you truly not remember your identity and gruesome crimes? Or did I deserve to be locked away because it was me all along? Did you really kill our mother with that bottle of pills you used to cover up the past?

Was I playing a mind game or finally shedding light on our truth?

Guess what?

I'm not going to tell. At least, not yet.

I've spent my entire life answering questions, having people probe into my mind, and looking for a way to connect the dots.

I'm done with that game.

It's time for a new one.

If I wasn't the killer before, I am one now.

Except, apparently, I didn't get the job done right.

I thought I had you too, that knife went in so smoothly, it was almost too easy. At least, easier than I expected it to be.

I guess I should have stabbed you a couple more times for some insurance, but I didn't think you'd live through the first stabbing. You were clearly weak; it was obvious from the moment you met me outside the institution.

Your eyes were so wide and innocent. The sadness that filled them when you'd heard I'd been left behind and forgotten. The guilt that was written so easily across your face. A monkey could have figured out how to manipulate you.

I truly tried to stifle the urge to kill you.

I just wanted you to get me out of the institution long enough that I could get things together to run away. Then I could get as far away from you, our past, and the family I never got to have and never look back.

Do you believe me?

Maybe I'm lying.

Maybe I had that knife under my pillow since the very night I came home, to a room that wasn't even mine. Maybe I had planned to kill you all along, every minute of every day since the day I knew what murder was. And if I am the true killer, I guess that was a very long time.

I'm laughing as I write this, I want you to know that.

Do you know why I'm laughing Sister?

It's because you don't know. You. Don't. Know. Anything.

I'm the only one that has the answers to your own life. And I don't have any plans of giving them to you. Yet.

But do you want to know about me? About where I went and what I'm doing?

Those answers I'll give you.

Do you know why?

Because I want you to know how easy it was to flee the first time I tried to kill you.

Oops- did you catch that?

Let me write that again. Because I want you to know how easy it was to flee the first time I tried to kill you.

That's right. I'm not done with you yet, Sister.

But it would have been no fun for me if I had just stayed in town and waited until the buzz around you died down.

I needed to let a little of your fame fizzle out before I could get to you again. Apparently, being nearly killed by your psychotic sister gave you a little local clout, didn't it?

Sad that it took that for anyone to have any interest in you.

I can see the puzzled look on your face in my mind, eyes wide as you're reading this thinking...if she wants to kill me so badly it must be because I was the one who should have been locked away, so what she said that night must be true.

An astute observation.

Though, it is only an observation.

Maybe I want to kill you because you never stuck up for me.

Or because I'm just jealous that you lived a life I didn't.

Or because I'm just a crazy killer.

Damn. Don't you wish you knew?

At first- you're going to want to turn this letter over to the police so they can look for clues to find me and take me back in and ensure your own safety.

You could do that.

But I can promise you this, if you do that, I'll know.

And then the letters will stop.

And they'll never find me.

And you'll never know when I'm coming.

But that's not why you're not going to turn these letters in.

No, we both know the real reason.

You want to know the truth, and I'm the only one who has it.

So, Sister, I suppose I'll say goodbye for now.

But don't worry, you'll be hearing from me soon.

Hugs and Kisses,

Kara

Chapter 3

Dear Sister,

How exactly did I get away?

This is the first of the questions I'm willing to answer for you because it is the simplest and I've actually found myself to be quite clever.

My face was plastered everywhere, police had barricaded off the streets, buses, highways, and everything else those slow pokes could think of.

But by the time they even found your bleeding body, I was long gone.

It's not like it was hard.

I hopped on the first rideshare app that I knew of and ordered a car. The car took me to the bus station where I boarded the bus that was going the farthest away from you. Then when that route ended, I went into the bathroom and used the hair dye I'd brought from the store near your house. A quick dye job, a change of clothes (yours actually- thanks for that), and some sunglasses, and back out into the world I went. A woman no one knew.

I took another bus, again to the farthest point possible, and that was pretty much that.

There was nothing wildly exciting. I have to admit my heart didn't even pick up speed as I went through these motions. The simplest person could have pulled this off.

Honestly, it amazes me how people even get caught nowadays. Like, you have to have not watched any True Crime documentaries ever.

Eventually, I figured I was far enough away that I could stop running, they wouldn't be looking halfway across the country for me. And even if they did, I proudly looked nothing like myself anymore.

Or you.

By the time I found a town to stay in, your face was plastered all over the news.

And they had given me a new name.

Sister Slayer

I found the alliteration satisfying.

But what was not satisfying was how the world seemed to glorify you.

For what? Being a victim?

Trust me, you're no victim.

But the world is looking at you and thinking That poor girl. How could her sister do something so cruel?

Pathetic.

Them. And you.

If only they knew the truth, the monster that you are. They wouldn't be pitying you; they'd be celebrating me.

They'd want you dead just as much as I do.

Just a few inches deeper with that knife and I would have made it happen. I'm still pissed at myself for that.

But not as pissed as I am with all the fame and glory you've gotten.

I've seen every interview, read every magazine article, and even read the rumors that they're making a movie based on you.

They're calling you a survivor.

It's pathetic, really, the way this world is fawning all over you.

You're not a survivor. You just happened to live when you didn't deserve it.

Do you know who is the real survivor?

It's me.

I'm the one who survived being left alone by my family.

I'm the one who survived Holden Lake Institute.

I'm the one who survived you.

And next time, I'll be sure I'm the only one who survives.

Hugs and Kisses,

Kara

Chapter 4

Dear Sister,

I was thinking about the time you broke your arm, do you remember that?

Look who I'm asking. You don't remember anything.

Even if you do remember the pink cast on your arm, I'm sure you don't remember how it happened. I'd have to guess that the only thing you'd remember is the distorted story that you made up yourself and that everyone believed.

I was the only one who knew the truth, but no one wanted to listen to me.

Why do you think that might be?

Well, let me tell you the story and then you decide.

It was one of those perfect spring days where the sun was shining and warm on your skin. The air smells fresh, like flowers and new grass. Everyone in the neighborhood seems to be outside.

Nigel was out on his driveway, playing basketball with his dad.

You remember Nigel, don't you? How could you forget? He is the key to all of this after all.

But that's a story for another day.

All the kids seemed to be outside playing that day, and you and I were eager to get out there too. We begged Mom all morning but she kept telling us that we needed to wait until Dad came home.

When his truck pulled into the driveway, we saw why Mom made us wait.

As we sat at the front window, we watched Dad pull two small bicycles out of his truck bed.

One was pink and one was purple.

You and I raced out of the front door as if we had firecrackers in our sneakers. We'd wanted bikes forever and this was the absolute best surprise.

"Who wants which one?" Dad called out.

I'll never forget his face when we finally got to him. He was just beaming. It's one of the last times I ever saw Dad look that happy.

I wanted pink, you knew I would want the pink one. Everything I owned was pink because that was my favorite color.

"I like the pink one!" you said before I could say anything.

So, Dad handed over the pink bike to you. And he handed me the purple.

I didn't blame him for not thinking of giving me the pink one, he was just so happy to be giving us bikes. I didn't argue, just accepted the purple one. I didn't think it mattered much anyway, a bike was a bike and I couldn't wait to start zooming all around the neighborhood on it.

We spent the afternoon outside, learning how to pedal and brake. Mom took pictures as Dad helped us get moving. Balancing wasn't hard with the training wheels on the back.

But I was better at it than you were, I was steadier and calmer. You wobbled more and got frustrated with it more easily. You wanted to be able to ride it like I could- but your coordination just wasn't as good as mine.

Mom and Dad kept saying you were determined, I knew you were mad. Dad kept working with you over and over again, trying to get you to get it right. Mom was fretting, worried you were going to get hurt.

Both of them kept their eyes on you instead of me, but I still didn't care. I had gotten a beautiful new bike and that's all I cared about.

I was riding like the wind (at least in my mind) up and down the driveway all afternoon. Unintentionally riding circles around you. Eventually, you did get the hang of it and we were both riding up and down the driveway.

"Can we please take the bikes down the street by ourselves?" you asked.

I wanted to ask the same question but I knew if you did they were more likely to say yes. They were always giving you whatever you wanted.

Mom looked at Dad and I could see she was worried. He shrugged.

"I used to play outside all the time by myself," he said. "We're in a safe neighborhood."

It's true- we were. There wasn't a better neighborhood for kids to grow up in than what we, (I guess I mean you- don't I) got to grow up in. Dad had no idea that the biggest danger was living right under his roof.

And despite leaving me like a piece of trash, he never did get that danger out of the house.

Do you think that's the real reason he left? Do you think somehow he knew the truth?

Once again, that is a story for another time....

Mom finally gave in to our pleas and Dad's comments.

"Fine, you can ride once down the sidewalk, and back. Don't cross the street. Just ride down, turn around, and come right back."

Both of us hopped on our bikes and took off. I think I heard her tell Dad to keep an eye on us but I can't be sure. I felt like I was riding like the wind; like nothing could touch me.

At one point I got ahead of you. You had practiced on the driveway but I was still better at riding than you were.

You called for me to slow down but I just couldn't, I didn't want to. I was flying and I'd never felt something so exciting before.

My little heart was racing and I know I had the largest smile on my face.

It was the last perfect moment I had.

Suddenly, I heard you scream. It wasn't the same way as when you were calling for me to slow down, it was different.

It was pain.

I pumped the brakes and got my bike to stop. I hopped off and turned around and saw that you weren't on your bike anymore.

You were on the ground, the pretty pink bike's handlebars bent, and you underneath.

I set my own bike on the ground and went running to my twin.

"What happened?" I asked.

Tears were streaming down your cheeks.

"I fell," was all you said.

You were cradling your arm, your knee was scraped, and you looked so sad in your helmet all cocked off to the side. I helped you up off of the ground and then picked up your bike.

I could tell the bike was pretty busted, and as I walked both of ours home and your hiccup crying slowed, I wondered how you could fall so hard with the training wheels still on.

When we got back home, Dad was outside in the front yard, watering the garden with the hose. He saw us and immediately dropped the hose and came running.

Seeing you were the injured one, he scooped you up and carried you inside. I put the bikes near the garage and followed you both into the house.

You were up on the countertop, while Mom fretted over your arm and cleaned up your knee.

"We'll probably have to take you to the hospital," she said.

"What happened?" Dad asked.

And that's when you looked at me, eyes locked on mine.

"I was riding and Kylie pushed me off the bike. She said she wanted the pink one."

Both Mom and Dad turned to look at me. I didn't say anything, I didn't even know what to say. That didn't happen, you had just made up that story and lied to them.

But the way they looked at me is forever in my mind.

They believed you.

And then nothing was the same ever again.

It was fitting when the doctor asked what color you wanted your cast- you picked pink.

I hadn't expected you to pick anything else.

I wonder what you're thinking of that story right now- are you trying to remember your cast or the bike?

Or do you still think I'm lying?

I bet your wrist still hurts when it rains.

Sister, I hope it pours on you tonight.

Hugs and Kisses,

Kara

Chapter 5

D*ear Sister,*

I can't tell you how exciting it is to be living on the outside.

Holden Lake is a prison for someone who doesn't belong there. Which clearly, I did not.

I couldn't pick what I wanted to wear or eat what I wanted to eat. I was on a schedule for everything I did. They told me when it was time to sleep, eat, go outside, exercise, read, socialize with other people, and everything else I did.

Do you know what that feels like?

Of course, you don't. You've spent your whole life living with total freedom. Just you and Mom, doing whatever you wanted whenever you wanted.

Maybe Holden is good for the patients who actually needed to be there, but that wasn't me.

It's crazy, being out here like this. I haven't felt this light since riding that purple bike for the first time.

I feel like I'm flying; like I'm free.

It was never fair that I was trapped in those walls. I was labeled a monster which I wasn't.

Even when I would go outside, I was still trapped. I'd lay in the grass and close my eyes, feel the sunshine on me, and pretend I was back home with my family. Sometimes I could get my mind to actually believe I was there.

Those were my favorite moments.

But as always, when my time outside was up and a nurse would come and get me to come back in, I was still at Holden Lake.

I could never keep the delusion up long enough.

I'm not living in a delusion anymore, I really am free.

Right now I'm staying somewhere temporary, but it's mine. No one tells me when to eat or sleep, I can come and go as I please.

I choose my own food, whatever I want! If I want pasta, I eat pasta. Chicken? I find somewhere to get chicken. There's no menu I have to stick to anymore.

I have my own clothes, my own books, and my own room.

It's funny, I'm telling you all of the things I have as if this would be some huge deal to you. But you've always had these things, you've had all of these things right at your fingertips your whole life.

But I bet you took them for granted.

I bet you took for granted going to sleep every night and not having to listen to a roommate sob.

Then again, I lived with you for those short couple of days. And I know you do your own crying at night, you don't need anyone to do it for you.

I think the next thing I'm going to do is get a job. It can't be that hard right?

Oh- except for the fact that if they run my name on an application I'm going to have a warrant out for my arrest.

Good thing I already have a fake ID. And a fake social security number. And a fake birth certificate.

It's amazing what you can pay people to do out here.

Outside of Holden Lake, I mean.

So yes, wish me luck Sister, I'm going to go job hunting tomorrow.

It's kind of exciting, isn't it? This start at a new life? A truly new beginning for me. Of course, yours isn't going to go the same way. You have to deal with the past before I'll ever let you have a future.

And even then Sister, I'm still not sure I'm going to let you have it.

I guess only time will tell.

Hugs and Kisses,

Kara

Chapter 6

D*ear Sister,*

I haven't written in a little while, have you missed me?

Or did you hope that I had decided to drop this little game we're playing?

Well, I suppose it is me who is playing it, not you.

Maybe you thought that I had gotten bored or decided to get on with my life.

I have decided to get on with my life but don't worry- I'm not bored of you yet.

I've just been so incredibly busy with my new and fabulous life that I haven't had time to write! But, tonight I decided my sister should get to hear my updates.

After all, if you can't share your fortune with your family, who can you share it with?

So, let me tell you just what has been happening out in this big beautiful world.

I've officially been able to begin my life in....oops...did you think I was going to tell you where I moved?

I will, one day, but that day isn't today.

Patience Sister.

Like I was saying....I've got an apartment, a cute one too. It's much bigger than any space I had at Holden and I adore having the privacy. It's wonderful not having people constantly around me; no staff or roommates to bother me when I would much rather be alone.

It sounds like a lonely existence, doesn't it? But after spending my entire life surrounded by people, loneliness is feeling an awful lot like freedom.

Plus, I get plenty of interaction at work.

Yes, you read that right, I have a job!

Isn't it wild?

An apartment and a job are all my own.

Oh, I don't know how people complain about working- I absolutely adore being out there in the working world.

Maybe I shouldn't give you this little clue, but I'm going to anyway- I got a job in a restaurant where I am a waitress.

I had to fib just a little to get hired since I have no job experience and certainly no waitressing experience, but I've picked it up quickly.

In fact, I have some customers who love me so much that they always request me as their server.

Can you believe it?

People love me, ME!

I make a living wage, plus excellent tips, and I even get a full meal of my choosing every shift I work.

It's incredible! How can anyone complain about a life like this?

I work as much as they let me; picking up extra shifts for the other servers just so I can be at the restaurant more often. Getting to be out in the world, talking to people, and even making friends, is a luxury so many people take for granted.

Honestly, I don't know why you've had such a sad little existence out in the world. Rather pathetic really when you see what the world has to offer.

I mean, do you even have a friend? Just one?

Sure, you have reporters, book deals, and producers coming after you- so I suppose that's something. But first of all, you didn't get that on your own- it's all because of me that you have that. And secondly, once the buzz dies down about you- which I'm sure will be coming any day now, you'll go back to your lonely, sad existence.

But me? My life is just beginning- and I don't see it slowing down any time soon. The future is going to keep getting bigger, brighter, and more exciting for me.

I never thought life could be this amazing.

Can I tell you one more thing? It's kind of a secret but I just have to tell somebody. And who better to tell than my sister?

I met a boy.

He works the restaurant with me- he's a bartender and is there almost every night. If I'm being fully honest, he's part of the reason that I pick up those extra shifts, just so I can spend a little extra time with him.

Let me tell you, he is like no one I've ever met before. Not that I have much to compare him to, but I just know inside of me that he's something special.

His name is Adam, and he is sweet and funny. He has this killer smile and this charm about him that is irresistible. All the girls at work are always talking to him and trying to get to the bar and flirt with him. We even have customers come in just to sit and talk with him, oh and those girls flirt with him constantly too.

But he doesn't seem interested in any of them.

I see the way he looks at me. It's different than the way he looks at them. And the way he goes out of his way to give me an extra smile or get my table's drink orders first, I think that he likes me too.

I want to tell him, maybe even see if he'd want to hang out sometime, but I'm so nervous! He's just so...perfect. I'm making a perfect life now, he doesn't need to know anything about my life before I arrived in his world, so just maybe I could fit into his somehow.

There is just one loose end I'll have to tie up.

And that, Sister, is you.

This is an unfortunate loose end because I'm rather enjoying getting to share all these sisterly secrets with you.

What a shame.

Well, I need to get ready for work now- Adam is working tonight so I always like to give myself a little extra time to get ready.

I'll write soon Sister, you can be sure of that.

Hugs and Kisses,

Kara

Chapter 7

*D*ear Sister,

What's this I've read about you getting brain surgery?

You just can't help yourself, can you? You have to keep yourself in the limelight at all times, don't you?

On the one hand, I should be happy about your desire to know what really happened. This surgery is supposed to help you remember the truth. And I should be relieved that I've gotten to you and made you see your world isn't what you think it is.

But on the other hand, it feels a little unfair because I want to be the one who wrecks your world with reality. Instead, you're going to let these doctors put probes inside of your head and mess around in there.

And then what will you do when you know the truth? What will you do when you see that you've been the liar all along? Are you going to admit it to the world- clear my name and set me free? Or, are you going to cover it up just like you always did and keep playing the victim?

It's funny, you would think that this type of story is a rarity. That innocent people don't get sent away for no reason. It seems like some crazy twisted plot or a movie or something, doesn't it?

Except, it's not.

And as I grew up in Holden Lake, I learned just how common it is. The stories that I heard inside of that place could send shivers up your spine. The things people were locked away for were more dangerous, and more terrifying than anything I did. Or anything they thought I did.

But if you've learned anything from me, it should be that the world isn't black and white. Some of those people were just like me. Nothing more than a story, no more threatening than a fly. And to be locked away so unfairly- the world painting you as some kind of monster that you know you're not- bonded us all in a way that you could never understand.

Inside those walls, so few of us were actually monsters.

We were simply...misunderstood.

As much as I'd longed for freedom my whole life, there has always been a part of me that was afraid of it.

See, on the inside, I knew who the real monsters were and who were just like me. But beyond those walls, I knew there were people like you. Walking around, acting so normal and innocent, hiding the true blackness inside of her.

It made me start to wonder when I finally got out, would I be able to tell the difference between the villains and the heroes?

Would I be able to spot a monster inside of someone by the way they tilted their head or smiled just a little too long?

Or, would I have to walk around in a world where my guard was always up and I was constantly looking over my shoulder?

I would ask you what your secret is, to making the world believe you're someone that you're not, but you have an unfair advantage.

You don't remember.

But you will, I just hope I get to finish telling you our story before they get to you.

I have to wonder when you do finally know the truth, how will you hide that monster inside?

We'll find out soon enough- one way or the other.

Hugs and kisses,

Kara

Chapter 8

Dear Sister,

I've given it some thought. Now that I know what a true coward you are, I've decided to take things up a notch, just a little. I've known since the day you let them take me to the institute that you were a chicken since you wouldn't even admit the truth to spare your own sister. But I always assumed it was because you wanted to save yourself, keep yourself on the outside of the institution walls, and keep living your devious little life.

Up until I saw you again, that was always what I believed.

I never knew the true coward that you were, one that was hiding the truth from yourself.

So, I got to thinking about this surgery. And I started doing a little research at the library.

And wow, even I didn't know you were this pathetic.

On the one hand, if the surgery works you finally won't be able to hide from the truth anymore.

On the other hand, if it doesn't, you won't remember anything at all.

Or maybe, that's what you truly want.

To not remember one thing about your past. Not me, Mom, your name, or the truth.

This brings me to my point, I'm going to have to get the truth out there much faster.

Because what fun would it be if it's the surgeons that finally make you remember and not me?

Today's little tale is one of a true psychopath, a serial killer if you will. Because now that you've killed Mom, you are one, aren't you?

Or is it killing three people that make you a true serial killer?

I can't quite remember.

Oh well, even if you're not a serial killer, you are still a psychopath.

When that pink cast was removed from your arm, things began to get back to normal. I had almost forgotten about that day entirely. Of course, when you're little, it's normal to do this, not when you're practically an adult.

As a kid, I didn't want to see what you were truly capable of. My sister had tried to turn my parents against me, had gotten hurt- maybe even hurt herself, and then blamed it on me. I didn't want to believe my sister could be that cruel.

It had to have been a mistake- something I had misunderstood at the time. And life seemed normal again so eventually, I didn't think about it anymore.

Until that fall.

As our neighborhood was a quiet one, it became more frequent for our parents to let us go play with some of the other kids on the street. After the bike incident, where Mom was nervous to let us go, she started to loosen the reins. I don't know if it was because we were with other kids our age, or if it was because she realized that despite her best efforts- she couldn't protect us from everything.

Little did she know she wasn't able to protect us from anything.

It's funny though, at least a little, that she died believing she did. You killed her while she still thought I was the killer. She went to her grave firmly believing she protected her innocent daughter from a tragic ending.

Well, she sure didn't protect you from a tragic ending, that's still coming. And she never once protected her innocent daughter.

It was a Saturday just like any other Saturday. The summer sun was not so hot and the leaves were losing their green in favor of the decaying colors of fall.

We'd been playing almost all day outside, bouncing from one backyard to the next. We played tag and hide and seek, climbed apple trees, and even had a mud fight. We were kids being kids.

At least, I was.

You, dear Sister, weren't having quite as much fun.

In fact, you almost never had the type of fun I had with the neighbor kids.

More often than not, you were like oil and water with them. When you were tagged out in a game, you would argue and scream until you either stormed home or the other kids would let you have your way.

The looks they gave you should have embarrassed us both, it was clear they thought there was something wrong with you. But I was used to your drama. It became normal in our house- even if Mom and Dad always thought I started it.

But the other kids never got used to it.

They never really wanted to play with you.

Do you know who they did want to play with?

Me.

I was the one they liked. I was the fun one. And you were a tag-along.

And what was funniest to me was that you didn't like playing with them anyway. You would only come along with me because Mom and Dad would tell you to.

If you had it your way, you'd have sat in your room all day.

By yourself.

Not even with me, your sister.

You were always happier when you were alone. Was it because you were happier by yourself or was it because you couldn't get along with anyone else? I don't actually know the answer to that.

But I never should have brought you along with me that day.

Or any day after.

We had been playing tag in between a set of houses. You were the tagger.

I'll admit, you were fast. When you were the tagger, we rarely had to play an extra round because you always would catch someone.

But an older girl was playing with us that day, her name was Gwen.

She was a little bigger, with long legs, and she seemed to be your target.

You easily could have caught anyone else who was playing, but you wanted Gwen.

It was like she was all you could see.

Our 'safe zone' was an old wooden picnic table. To be safe from the tagger, all you had to do was touch the table and you were safe.

Gwen was mere feet away.

Are you starting to remember? Can you see it in your mind? Her blonde hair flew behind her as you chased her. The laugh that bubbled up from her because she had no idea who she was dealing with.

I remember it as if it was just yesterday.

Then again, most of the memories from our childhood hit me like that. As if I'm still living them each day.

I remember watching you chase Gwen, knowing that you wouldn't be able to catch up to her. I remember the sinking feeling I had in my stomach knowing that when you didn't catch Gwen when she made it safe, none of us were going to be safe.

Just when her fingertips were about to brush the table, I saw you do it. You moved toward the side of her just a little and stuck your foot out enough. I don't know how you were able to reach her that way when you couldn't even tag her, but you did.

And she tripped.

And she fell.

And she banged her head on the picnic table.

They say a head wound always bleeds badly. Sometimes it makes it hard to know if it's a bad injury or just a little cut.

When Gwen picked her head up, there was no guessing.

Blood was already pooling down her face.

Matting her blonde hair that moments before had been flying freely behind her.

Crimson drips were seeping into her clothes.

The crying didn't start right away, not until the realization finally hit her of what had happened.

"You did this on purpose!" she yelled at you in between sobs.

You shrugged. "It was an accident. I was only trying to tag you," you said.

The ice in your voice still snakes through my veins sometimes.

If I were a betting girl, I'd say it still snakes through hers too.

Gwen sprung up, which I can't imagine would have been easy with the blood in her eyes, and ran home.

She never came out to play with us again.

I would see her playing with the other kids, but never with us.

Or at least, she didn't want to play with you.

Gwen's mom called that night.

I couldn't hear what she was saying, but I could hear our parents.

They were defending you, as always.

Saying that we had just been playing.

Telling her that it had been an accident.

That Kara wouldn't hurt anyone.

Did you catch that part?

Kara wouldn't hurt anyone.

See, we were little.

And we were twins.

And Gwen didn't know us very well.

And in her hysteria, she couldn't tell us apart.

Do you know what the worst part was?

It wasn't the blood or the screaming that was stuck inside of my brain, and it wasn't even the fact that she said it was me that had tripped her.

It was that when Mom and Dad had to defend me, I could hear it in their voices.

They were defending me, but they didn't believe their own defense.
They thought I was guilty.
And that was one step closer to the end for me.
And now, for you.
Think hard about this one Sister.
I hope that when you go to sleep tonight, all you see is blood.
Sweet dreams Sister.
Hugs and Kisses,
Kara

Chapter 9

Dear Sister,

This is all your fault! Why can't I ever have anything good? Why does the world punish good people like me and praise the evil in the world?

Your press coverage hasn't died down one bit like I thought- in fact, the closer it gets to your surgery, the more you seem to get. Did I read in an update that you signed up with a film company that wants to document your surgery?

I bet you're going to get a big chunk of change for that- not to mention that you're going to get even more fame. Even more sympathy. Even more praise.

I can't fucking believe it.

You're a monster! How do people not see that? How are you so good at hiding your real self?

I just don't understand!

Reward after reward.

And me?

I'm an innocent victim in all of this and I am the one who keeps losing!

Do you want to know what happened?

I. Lost. Everything.

My job, Adam, my friends.

I have nothing left.

And why is that?

Because I spent my entire life locked away in an institute and NO ONE prepared me for what it would be like to have to be on the outside and interact with people that are not like me.

And just like everything else that has gone wrong in my life, I blame you for that.

Adam is not who I thought he was, not at all. I was so stupid for liking him, for thinking he could like a girl like me.

And before you even start to think I'm looking for your pity, Sister, I'm not. Instead- I want you to know how much you've ruined my life. That no matter how far away I get, no matter how much I try to change my life- you and Holden Lake have ruined me.

Are you thinking to yourself that it's probably good Adam doesn't like a girl like me?

Do you even care about what happened?

I'll tell you what happened- so you can add one more thing to the list of reasons why I'm coming for you.

I was so sure Adam liked me. Honestly. I gushed about that jerk in my last letter, saying that he talks to me a little extra when I'm working. And that he gets my drinks a little quicker than he gets everyone else's.

On my last shift, I was telling Rebecca, a co-worker who I actually thought was my friend, that I had a crush on Adam. I even admitted that I thought he liked me too.

"Go ask him out," she said to me.

We were supposed to be in the middle of a dinner rush but it was quiet last night. Rebecca, that bitch, and I were preparing silverware up at one of the empty tables.

"I can't, I don't know how to ask out a guy," I said to her.

She rolled her eyes at me and laughed, but I thought it was playful.

"Come on, haven't you ever asked out a guy before?"

Of course, people don't know about my real history, only the one I've made up for them.

"Not really, I never really needed to," I told her.

It was the truth, I never asked anyone out at Holden Lake. But that's because we weren't allowed to date there.

See? Even when I'm hiding my real life, I still tell the truth.

"I think you should go up to him and just ask him out."

I looked over at the bar and Adam was laughing at something I couldn't hear. His dark stubble made his smile even brighter. And those dark eyes nearly danced. I watched him as he moved, effortlessly, between the few scattered conversations at the bar.

Adam turned and caught my eye and directed that perfect bright smile towards me.

I blushed, I know I did.

"Do you think I should?" I asked her.

She nodded and giggled.

"Make the move, what do you have to lose? I've heard him talking about you, he likes you. I'm sure of it."

Can you guess what I did after that?

I took a deep breath and I walked up to the bar. I felt Rebecca's eyes on me and looking back I even think she was still giggling while I made my way up there.

"Hey Adam," I said.

I was shaking, Sister.

He smiled at me and my knees went weak.

"Did you have an order I missed?" he asked and gestured toward where the order tickets were printed out.

But I shook my head. My tongue felt thick like I couldn't move it in my mouth. I was so nervous. I'd talked to Adam plenty of times. Well, maybe not plenty. But at least once a night since I was hired.

I tried to steady myself. Tried to make myself seem as normal as possible. I mean, it wasn't like he hadn't been talking with me too all those nights. One of us just had to suck it up and make the move.

"I was wondering, what are you doing tonight, after your shift?"

His eyes burned into mine and my palms got sweaty.

When he didn't say anything, I just kept talking.

I thought about Rebecca's words and remembered that I didn't have anything to lose.

"I thought that maybe when you're done, we could hang out?"

I stood there, like a fool, just waiting for him to tell me what he wanted to do after work.

It didn't even occur to me to notice that the longer I stood there, the more his smile faded. Until eventually it became awkward.

I looked around and noticed that everyone that was sitting at the bar was trying to find anything else to look at other than me.

Behind me, I could hear Rebecca's giggles turn to laughter.

This time my cheeks blushed but for a whole other reason.

Adam moved towards me but couldn't look me in the eye.

"I'm sorry. I'm just...not interested in you that way. I think we should keep this strictly a working relationship," he said to me.

Tears burned in my eyes when he said that. Rebecca's laughter erupted at his words and I even heard a few snickers from the people at the bar.

I didn't say anything. I couldn't say anything. I'd never felt that kind of embarrassment before.

I've felt a lot of things in my life- pain, anger, sadness, loneliness, confusion...but embarrassment isn't one of them.

I left that night, I can't ever go back.

Rebecca wasn't my friend- she's a bitch who played a dirty trick on me.

Adam wasn't a guy who was interested in me- just a boy playing games.

And if those two things aren't what I thought, then maybe nothing is.

Maybe nothing about this outside world is what I thought it was.

And that, dear Sister, brings me back to you.

It always comes back to you.

If you hadn't gotten me locked away, I may have realized what was happening. That people wear masks, play games, and get off by hurting others.

I would understand the way the world works and the way it doesn't.
But because of you- I don't know those things.
And I'm starting to wonder if I ever will. If I'll ever be able to fit in.
Or if no amount of freedom can free me from what you've done.
Please, add that to the list of reasons that I can't wait to come back for you.

Hugs and Kisses,
Kara

Chapter 10

*D*ear Sister,
I've been taking it easy on you.
Just like everyone has your entire life.
But I've decided I'm done.
Why should I take it easy on you?
You've got everything you could want.
The world is worshipping you.
And the ones who aren't, they are feeling sorry for you.
Everyone wants to protect you.
And the fame and money you are getting from this will set you up for life.
It's sickening.
Not as sickening as you.
Let's try for another memory, shall we?
This one is a damn doozy.
Do you know why you don't have any pets?
I believe I asked you that one night while I was living with you.
When you were crying from your dreams, or nightmares I would bet.
And you asked if a cat was running in your house.
I have to admit, I was proud of myself for that one.
It was pretty damn funny.
It wasn't easy to stay so calm and collected when I was messing with your mind so well.
And so easily.
You never did answer my question that night. Do you know why you never had a pet?

I can tell you why.

It's because of me.

Well, you, technically.

But just like with everything else, Mom and Dad thought it was me.

I had a kitten once.

Pepper.

He was a stray.

A tiny gray furball that was speckled with flecks of black.

Pepper was a perfect name for him.

I'd found him in a bush in Mom's flowerbed which was drying up from the fall ending and the cold of winter beginning.

It took a lot of begging for me to keep him. I had to promise to take care of him all the time. To change his litterbox. To do extra chores to pay for his food.

The house had been a little rocky for months. First your broken arm. Then the drama with Gwen. Then just little things, here and there. Small confusions, lies, and fights made the house stand slightly on edge.

It wasn't a fun time in the house.

Pepper seemed to make things brighter. And with the bleak feel of winter on its way, our family needed it.

You and I both loved Pepper. And as a rambunctious kitten- Mom and Dad found him cute too.

Or maybe they didn't.

Maybe they were just so happy to have some calm, something positive, in the house after so much chaos.

But for a couple of weeks, things seemed to be going better.

Every night Pepper would cuddle on my bed with me.

He loved me more than you.

And you couldn't stand that.

Just like you couldn't stand when anyone liked me more.

Or when I got something you wanted.

There was only one night that you tried to get Pepper to stay with you in your bed.

"He's my cat too!" you yelled.

Mom and Dad, surely hoping to keep the peace for a while longer, decided that Pepper had stayed with me enough nights.

It was your turn.

Do you know how they say that animals can sense good and evil?

Pepper meowed at the door all night long, scratching at the doorway.

I wanted to get out of bed and get him. He never did this when he was with me.

But I didn't.

I stayed in bed.

I let him stay with you.

I never should have done that.

In the morning, I couldn't wait to see Pepper.

I wanted to cuddle him and play with him. I'd missed him and his warm spot on my bed.

But when I got up, I saw your door was already open.

When I peered my head inside, you weren't in your bed.

I went downstairs, thinking you'd be at the breakfast table.

And I was right, you were.

Sitting at the table. Swinging your feet that couldn't yet touch the ground.

Just like me.

I looked around the kitchen, expecting to see Pepper scurrying about, chasing after a toy like usual. But I didn't see him.

"Where's Pepper?" I asked you.

You tilted your head and looked at me confused.

"You came and got him last night," you said to me.

Just then, Mom came into the kitchen. Pepper's empty food bowl sat on the ground.

"Did anyone feed Pepper today?" she asked.

"Kara came and got him in the middle of the night. He wouldn't go to sleep," you said.

Before I could tell her that that wasn't true, Mom turned her questions to me.

"So where is he? I haven't seen him or heard him racing around all morning."

Just like me, we had all gotten used to Pepper's cute antics.

Without him, the house felt wrong. Even more off than it had been for the past few months.

There was an unease in the air.

"I...I don't know. I didn't come to get him last night," I said.

But of course, with everything that had happened lately, Mom's face told me she didn't believe me.

We looked all through the house that morning. Under tables, behind furniture, and even in our shoes.

Yours had a little mud on them.

I noticed.

So, I put on my shoes and went outside.

I looked all around the yard.

But there was no little Pepper.

I decided to check the garden- the same place I had found him.

If the blood wasn't so bright, I may not have ever known he was there.

I raced to him, his poor little body, my poor baby.

I scooped him up in my hands and watched as his insides slipped through my fingers.

Vomit rose in my throat, but it was the scream that made its way out of me.

Pepper had been crudely cut open from his throat all the way down his body. His blood, a pool underneath him on the frozen ground. Sticky and still warm, not yet soaked into the earth. His insides were now on the outside.

Mom and Dad both came running to me.

I sobbed.

I'd never cried so hard in my life.

Not Pepper.

Not my little kitten.

Not the only little thing I had in my life that I loved. That loved me.

"What did you do?" Dad screamed at me.

He grasped at Pepper's limp little body.

I saw his face turn green.

Mom turned her back to me.

You never even came outside.

How did they think I could do something like this?

They knew I loved Pepper. They knew I was the one who wanted Pepper so desperately.

But they also knew what you told them- I went and got him from your room.

And they knew what they saw- me holding the bloody body of my kitten who had been ripped apart.

"Did you let him outside?" Mom asked, tears filling her eyes as Dad wrapped Pepper's body in a towel. "Do you think an animal got to him?" she asked my dad.

The tone was hopeful. She wanted me to say yes. I had let him outside. She wanted it to be a harmless accident.

Just like Gwen.

Just like the bike.

I tried to nod, I tried to lie. Because even at a young age, I knew that I was going to get the blame for this no matter what I said.

"This isn't done by an animal," he answered with a growl. "This is the slice from a knife."

Mom didn't say another word.

Dad took Pepper to the backyard where he spent the morning digging at the frozen ground.

But do you know what no one noticed? The thing no one even questioned?

Why I would have gotten Pepper from your room in the first place? And if I had, what was my motive for killing him? Why would I want to kill the one thing I loved more than anything?

There is one more thing, Sister, that no one questioned- that no one seemed to notice.

While Mom was disgusted and Dad was digging, I was sobbing inconsolably.

You sat at the table, pouring yourself another bowl of cereal, and swinging your feet.

Without a care in the world.

So, I will answer that question for you, the one I asked you that night at your house.

Doesn't it seem strange you never had a pet?

The reason is probably because it was too awful of a memory for Mom, and something she probably didn't want you to have to remember.

What I hope though, deep down, is that somehow, she always questioned how you kept eating, unbothered, when our kitten had just been gutted.

And if I get my way, I'll gut you just like you did to him.

Pepper was an innocent kitten. You, Sister, are the farthest thing from innocent.

And I can't wait to see your insides.

Hugs and Kisses,

Kara

Chapter 11

D*ear Sister,*
       I. Hate. You.
Do you know what you just made me do?
I tried. I tried really damn hard.
I tried to survive out here.
After all of those years locked away, I believed that I would be just fine out here.
But apparently- being locked away and told you're a monster for your whole life will make you one.
Work kept calling me, asking when I was coming back. I kept telling them I was sick but they insisted they needed me to get back into work or they would have to hire someone else.
So, I tried to do what normal people do in the outside world.
I went back.
And they laughed at me.
And Adam wouldn't look at me.
And the girls whispered about me- calling me dramatic.
Fuck them all.
I couldn't stay. I burst back through the restaurant doors yelling behind me that I quit.
How do people live in a world like this?
How do people mess with others, make jokes about them, and then just act as if it's nothing?
These thoughts- they've been stewing in me. Building up.
Just like when I was in Holden.

And alone in my apartment; with no friends, no job, no Adam, no hope, I didn't know what to do.

At least at Holden, I was never alone. Not like I am now.

In my apartment, I felt like a caged animal. I paced back and forth, trying to understand how I got it so wrong.

Do you know what conclusion I came to?

I'm not to blame for this.

I was doing so well in my new life- until Adam. Until Rebecca.

The more I thought about it, the more I couldn't stand it.

My whole life started unraveling before my eyes and I felt this burning inside of me.

Searing anger and pain.

I needed to do something, I needed to let the anger out. Or at the very least, I needed to find a way to straighten things out.

Adam liked me- I was sure he did.

So, what went wrong?

Sister, I needed to know.

When I knew Adam's shift would be ending, I went to the restaurant and waited in the back parking lot by his car.

I needed to settle this. You know, for my own peace of mind.

When Adam came walking out, I pictured that he would see me and smile. It had been about a week since I'd been at work, almost two since the whole embarrassing ordeal.

But when he saw me- he didn't look happy. He didn't smile at me.

Instead, he looked...confused.

"Hey," I said.

I tried to be bright and smiley like I'd seen the other girls act.

But he didn't smile back.

"Um...hi...what are you doing here?" he asked me.

That made the anger in me burn brighter- the fact that he didn't seem happy to see me. The fact that he looked like I didn't even belong there.

"I just...I just wanted to know what happened. I mean, I thought you liked me? You seemed to when we would talk."

Adam rolled his eyes and took a step closer to his car door, where I was standing.

"I'm nice to everyone- it's part of the job. It's how I get tips, you should know that. You've worked in the restaurant industry."

He reached into his pocket for his keys.

"It just seemed like you liked me..."

"Liked you? I barely know you. You'd come up to the bar and get your drinks and barely even speak. Just kind of stood there; it was weird. But I talk to anyone though."

His keys in his hands, he moved so close to me I could smell his cologne mixed with the sweat of a hard shift done.

"Do you mind?" he asked and gestured for me to move so he could get into his car.

But I couldn't move. I felt frozen to the pavement, despite the heat of the night.

Who was this guy? So rude, arrogant, and not even close to the nice guy I thought he was.

Was he telling me the truth? That all of his kindness was just an act? A way to get extra tips, or get girls to fall for his charm.

Just like I did.

And you know what I realized?

This outside world is full of liars.

Like you are.

Like Adam was.

Did you catch that?

I did move away from his car. But I couldn't let him get away with being a fake, being a liar.

It's liars like you people that ruin the world for the rest of us.

When I moved, I bumped his shoulder- just a little. Just enough.

His keys hit the pavement and I kicked them just a little out of his reach.

Here's another lesson I've learned- people never assume the worst.

And they're never ready for it.

"Sorry," I said and bent down to get his keys.

Before I could stop myself, I jammed the keys hard through the side of his throat.

Those beautiful eyes went wide. The last bit of life flashed through them as the blood pooled out of his neck, down that dark stubble.

I let go before the blood could soak into the sleeve that was covering my hands because you know- fingerprints dear Sister.

He reached for me, desperate and scrambling. And damn I almost held him up, I almost tried to help.

I wished somewhere inside of me I could find mercy.

But then I remembered you, looking at me in that exact same pitiful way when I stabbed you.

And I knew that I had to let him die.

People like him, people like you, don't deserve to keep walking this earth playing games and hurting others.

People like Rebecca don't either.

And one day, I'm sure I'll be able to get her back too.

Just like you.

Hugs and Kisses,

Kara

Chapter 12

Dear Sister,

I will NEVER FORGIVE YOU!!!

My life will never be a real life. Not like you have, not like anyone has.

I can't function out here.

I don't know what I'm supposed to do- how I'm supposed to act.

How I'm supposed to hold in this anger when the world is awful outside of the walls I'm used to?

And why is that?

Because you got me locked away.

You played your little game and manipulated your way into your perfect life. Which you still managed to fuck up. And you're the one coming out on top with fame and money.

And I just killed a man in a parking lot.

At least this time, I know he's dead.

Not like when I left you, believing you'd die and yet you lived.

I made sure he was dead before I left that parking lot.

His death isn't why I'm so angry.

He deserved it.

What I'm mad about is the fact that I had just started over. And it was going so well.

And now I can't stay here.

I mean, they're never going to suspect me.

Again, true crimes come in handy.

My hood was up.

I left no prints.

And I didn't even work there anymore.

He didn't even make a sound when I stabbed him, so by the time he was found dead- I was long gone.

I was just a shadow in the night.

But there will be investigations and there is only a matter of time before someone realizes who I am. If they dig hard enough.

I was happy. For the first time since they dumped me off at Holden, I was happy.

You wouldn't know what that feels like, would you? You take your life for granted. Sister, you have no idea how good you've had it. Or how good you have it now.

Just thinking about that; that you live in your pathetic bubble whining about your life that you've wasted and I am the one who has to keep running....it's making that white hot anger bubble inside of me.

Poor Adam, it really wasn't his fault.

And when Rebecca drinks her drink tonight at the bar, it won't be her fault either.

It's yours.

All of these lives are ruined because there is a monster on the loose.

And it isn't me.

There's only one way to put a stop to this.

And that's to put an end to you.

I'll be seeing you soon Sister.

Hugs and Kisses,

Kara

Chapter 13

I fold the last letter Kara sent me and stash it back in the large envelope with the rest of them.

She's killed again.

Maybe more than once, if that drink hit Rebecca the way Kara made it sound like it would.

I shiver at the thought.

At least two more innocent lives are gone, and how many others are ruined, because of our family secret.

And the worst part of it all is I still don't know what the secret was.

Kara still seems as confident as ever that she didn't belong in Holden Lake Institute.

And everything after that; her anger, her killing, her ruined life, she has blamed on me.

I get up off the couch and stare for a moment at the spot in the room where Kara left me to die a little over a year ago.

She didn't succeed then but I know if she's given another chance, she isn't going to mess it up.

And according to her letters, she is ready to try again.

The last letter arrived just a week ago. Based on that timeline, she could be arriving anytime.

I don't know if it's the wine, or the letters, or the fact that I am a chicken shit who is afraid to go under the knife. But I take my cell phone out of my pocket and call the hospital.

It's the answering service that picks up which is a relief because I don't know what I would say if it was my actual doctor.

As it is, I find it hard to get the words out and I stutter my way through the point of my call.

"I have an appointment tomorrow, a surgery scheduled for the morning," I say to the woman answering the call.

"Are you calling to check the time?" she asks.

I can hear her tapping on a keyboard on the other end of the phone. Presumably bringing up tomorrow's surgery schedules.

"No...actually...I have to call and...postpone," I say.

"And what is your name?" she asks.

"Kylie Heston," I answer.

I picture her typing my name into a database as the line stays silent.

"Oh, Kylie," she says when she realizes who I am and what my procedure is. "Maybe before you postpone the procedure, you should talk to your surgeon in the morning?"

I know she's trying to talk me out of canceling- this is a groundbreaking surgery.

And for a moment, I think about telling her that she's right, that I should talk to my surgeon in the morning about my nerves.

But this isn't about nerves.

This is about a hell of a lot more than that.

This is about life and death.

Well, life or death.

Because I have a bad feeling that at the end of all of this....one of us isn't making it out alive.

And I need it to be me that survives.

I can't take the chance that sticking probes in my brain might erase all of me.

If the surgery backfires and I don't get my memory back, then I may never see Kara coming.

"No, I have to cancel," I tell her more firmly.

"Can I at least have a reason why? I'm sure he'll want to know."

"Because something is coming back to me, and I need to take the time to know what it is," I say.

I assure her I'll call back when I've gotten things under control and I'm ready for the procedure.

What I don't tell her, what I'm not going to tell anyone, is that it's my sister that's coming back to me. And if I don't figure out the truth, I'll never make it out alive.

With my surgery canceled, I know that I need a new plan. I need answers. Not the ones that Kara is giving me. And not ones that I get from having probes scramble my brain.

Real answers.

There is only one way I know to get those. One place that has to hold all of our sisterly secrets.

Holden Lake Institute.

And instead of surgery, that's where I'll be headed tomorrow.

Dear Sister, don't worry- I'll be ready for you.

III

GOODBYE SISTER

Chapter 1

Kylie

As it turns out, it's not so easy to cancel a groundbreaking surgery that is being filmed, paid for, and studied.

Waking up in the morning, I've got about a dozen missed calls from the surgeon, the doctor, the film crew, and everyone else under the sun it seems.

"Kylie, we need to talk about this. This surgery could truly do wonders for you and the field of science. Call me back as soon as you get this," my surgeon said.

"Kylie, I know our session didn't go perfectly the other day but you've been looking forward to this operation and I'm concerned about your sudden change of mind. Call me as soon as you get this," my therapist said.

"Kylie, there has been a lot of money, time, and effort that has been put into this documentary. And I need to remind you that you did sign a contract. You've been paid a portion already for the interviews you did but you don't receive the rest until the surgery is complete. And on top of that, the contract does state that you would not be backing out of the surgery for anything other than health reasons. Call me back as soon as you get this," my film director said.

I put my phone down and let the heaviness of it all sink into me.

This is my own fault, I know that. I should have read all of those letters beforehand. I probably should have told my therapist too.

Instead, each time I got one of those stupid letters, I'd hide it away and pretend it didn't exist, hoping that it would be the last one. But there was always some part of me that knew that if the letters stopped it was going to be for a reason.

And not a good one.

So, why didn't I look at them? Why was I such a chicken?

I'm confident that there is a deep-rooted answer inside of me somewhere but the reality is, when your long-lost twin sister tries to stab you to death- anything that has anything to do with her is going to terrify the shit out of you.

So, why didn't I go to the police?

That's a harder one to answer. And if I did a deep dive into my thoughts, I may not like what I find. Which is probably why I've avoided thinking about it. Maybe I didn't want her to get caught. Maybe I knew if I told the police the letters would stop. Maybe I always knew one day that I'd open them to get answers.

If I had been brave enough, these are all the things I would have thought about well before the night before my surgery.

Instead, I am having to think about all of that now.

And I can't say I'm any closer to answers. Still.

I know what Kara put in the letters. I must have stayed up all night reading and rereading them. Trying to dissect each story, each word, and find a truth or a memory in any of it.

But I still don't have a clue.

Any thought or memory that starts to pop into my mind makes me question if it's a real memory or if it's one that Kara has now planted inside me.

My mind is like an empty black pit. Each time I try to reach inside to find something, nothing is there.

It's like when you reach a handout to catch a fly. You know the fly is there and you move as quick as you can to catch it in your fist. You think you finally have it but when you open your fist, it was never there to begin with. You never caught the fly.

It's likely a stupid analogy, but it's all I can come up with. Because as hard as I try, I keep coming up empty-handed.

Kara's letters didn't do anything but put more confusion into my life.

I know the answers are buried inside of me somewhere, they have to be. This is why I was so sure that I was ready for the brain surgery because I was desperate to know the truth.

But how can I do it now when Kara could be on her way to me at any moment?

She's killed before. Hell, she tried to kill *me* before.

She's going to try it again.

But if I go under that knife, and the surgery fails, if I wake up not knowing anything, I won't be able to protect myself. I'll be a deer, unaware that the hunter is aiming for me.

I'm not ready to die.

Or at least. I'm not going to go without a fight.

There's a sickening feeling in the pit of my stomach that there is only one of us who is going to make it out of this mess.

And it has to be me.

Screw the contract, the money, the surgery...I don't have a choice.

It's life or death and I can't risk losing what little advantage I have.

Stretching the tension from my body, I roll out of bed and know what I have to do.

I'm a woman on a mission.

The first call I make is to the director.

It's early in the morning but he answers my call on the second ring. I'm sure he's awake pacing the floor, wondering what the hell he is going to do without the medical star of his documentary.

"Kylie, what's going on?"

I can hear the panic in his voice and I want to reassure him. But I know that I can't.

"I canceled the procedure last night. I know it isn't what you want to hear but I can't go through with it."

I try to keep my answer simple and to the point but I noticeably put a little fear into my voice. Maybe if he thinks I'm afraid then he'll let me off the hook. Who wouldn't be terrified and second-guessing having brain surgery?

I mean, I *wasn't*, but he doesn't need to know that.

"Kylie, we need to discuss this." His voice is gentle like he's trying to coax a kitten out of hiding.

"There isn't anything to discuss. If I change my mind and am ready to do this at some point, I will reach back out to you."

"That's not the way this works. You can't just cancel this without giving us anything. This was going to be a groundbreaking procedure. Do you even know how much time and money has been spent making this documentary? I told you in the voicemail, you signed a contract."

"I understand that but this is my body and my health. And I'm not going to let someone poke around in my brain just for your entertainment." It really isn't fair that I'm getting so feisty with him, he doesn't have any idea why I've changed my mind.

And I am kind of screwing him over.

"Kylie, did you read the contract before you signed it?"

I had told them that I'd had Mr. O'Neal look over the contract, but in reality, I'd skimmed it myself and signed. At that point, it felt like the whole world had already been watching me. The survivor of the Sister Slayer, what was one more thing? Besides, this way they'd pay for the surgery, the aftercare, and anything else I'd need, plus a check for my time.

It isn't like I need the money, but with no idea what the future holds- it's better to be safe than sorry.

Which is still the motto I'm going by.

"I read the contract," I lie. I've gotten good at lying, although admittedly I'm not always sure I know when I'm doing it anymore.

"Then you're aware that by not going through with the operation, you have to give back the money we've already paid you and you are liable for the rest of the loss as well."

My stomach suddenly starts to turn when it dawns on me what he's saying. But just for clarification....

"Meaning, what exactly?"

"Meaning everything that has been spent could be your responsibility to pay back. On top of that, anything the studio feels that it lost out on would be up to you to repay as well. That's a hell of a lot of money in legal fees alone, on top of what you'll pay. Why didn't you know this when you signed?"

I want to kick myself- I really should have called Mr. O'Neal.

"So...what am I supposed to do now?"

Panic and fear truly are rising in me now. I picture myself after surgery, not even knowing who I am, trying to restart a life as someone new, not knowing I should be constantly looking over my shoulder.

My sister wants me to be punished. And she isn't going to stop until she feels vindicated.

I hear Larry sigh on the other end of the line. Frustration mixed with sympathy.

"I'll tell you what. I'll give you a couple of days to sort out whatever it is you need to do. Call your doctor, your therapist, or whoever it is you need to talk to. If you still want to back out of this, well, then I'll transfer you to our legal team and won't ask you again to change your mind. But if you want to do this, then we're still here and ready."

Tears prick at my eyes. I know he doesn't mean to threaten me like that, in fact, the whole team has been amazing to me during all the interviews and everything. But I still live in the real world, not my little bubble. And decisions all have consequences.

If I do the surgery, I may wake up unprepared for Kara's return.

If I don't do the surgery, I won't have any chance of remembering anything about my life and I'll be in the legal battle of the century.

I don't have a choice.

"Fine. Give me a couple of days and I'll be ready."

I hang up the phone with a gut feeling that in a matter of days, this will all be over.

One way or another.

Chapter 2

Kara

I don't even know what I'm throwing in my bag, I'm just trying to fit in as much as I can.

Panic is flooding me and I don't know what I'm doing.

Clothes, a toothbrush, my identity (though I have to clearly get a new one of those now), just the necessities.

I don't have time to make this nice and neat.

Last time I had the murder planned out along with my perfect escape. Everything had been so thought out when I had planned Kylie's murder that I don't even think my heart rate ever climbed. I stayed calm and even throughout the whole thing.

But this...these murders I hadn't planned.

I don't even like that I have to call these murders...they're more like...accidental killings.

Stabbing Kylie was supposed to be a murder. I meant to do that. I craved ripping that knife into her insides and letting her life drain from her body.

But killing Adam in the parking lot...I didn't mean to do that. I didn't want to do that. I can't exactly say the key slipped right into his neck, but it was an impulse. Like shoplifting a candy bar while you are hungry. I've done that a couple of times, and I've seen others do it too. It's an impulse, but you don't really mean to do it.

That's what it felt like in that parking lot.

If I have to come clean, I suppose I can admit that killing Rebecca was a *little* planned. I did have to secure the drug, find what bar she was at, slip it in her drink, and then slip out without being seen. But I didn't know for sure it would actually kill her. There was a chance that it was just going to make her feel like shit, knock her out, and then regret her decisions in the morning.

I must have bought an extra high dose.

Whoops.

I didn't even know she died until I saw it on the news.

Which is why I'm packing.

Two dead bodies were found, both with a connection to each other. Crime shows have taught me plenty and one of the things I know for sure is that the first place they're going to start looking is with the people who knew them both.

And I'm on that list.

So, I have no choice but to pack up and get out as fast as possible. Before they knock on my door and I find myself in front of police officers who might recognize me because of my little incident with Kylie.

It's been a while since I ran away from that mess, but with her face constantly plastered all over the news, and resurfacing with this damn documentary and surgery, I imagine it wouldn't take a genius to notice that I look awfully similar to her.

I'm not going down for two murders and one attempted murder.

Especially when none of this is my fault.

When the police finally make their way to placing me into this murder puzzle, I'll be long gone. The apartment will look abandoned, it will all look suspicious. And if I had the time, I'd get it all cleaned up. I'd make sure everything was in order, wipe my presence from this life I'd built, and tie a neat little bow on it.

But I just don't have the time for this shit.

I was unprepared to have to be on the run again.

Scanning my apartment, I give a last look around.

My heart spasms in my chest a little, and I think it's pain. Sadness.

I'd worked so hard to start a new life.

I'd gotten out of Holden. I'd found a job. I thought I had found friends. I had one loose end to handle- and that was Kylie. But I'd found enjoyment in the game I'd been playing of sending her letters, so even she wasn't an issue for me lately.

And now I had to give it all up.

Stupid bitch. This is all her fault.

If Kylie had been able to just admit she was wrong, to clear my name, to fix my life just one time, then none of this would have happened.

Two people would still be alive. Hell, I'd even have my own life that I didn't need to keep running from.

And if she had owned up to her mistakes, she wouldn't have to be paying for them. At least not from me.

I'm going to have to make her pay sooner than I realized.

I can't wait.

But for now, I grab my quickly packed bags and go to my front door.

I've left no pictures, no address, no personal information at all. I've done my best to wipe my fingerprints and get rid of any evidence I existed. I'll be some girl that used to work at the restaurant, that everyone vaguely remembers but no one can pinpoint.

It hurts though, to have to walk away from everything I had.

Again.

With a final look back, I walk through my apartment door and close it behind me. Shutting out any chance I had at a new life.

At first, sending the letters to Kylie was mostly for my amusement. I knew I'd decide one day what to do with her. But I know now that there is no moving on until Kylie is taken care of.

I guess I will be seeing my sister sooner than I had planned.

And this time I won't miss. This time, it's for good.

Chapter 3

Kylie

I have to think and I'm going to have to get creative.

I can't give myself the answers, and it seems everyone has a version of the truth about what happened back when Kara and I were kids.

So, who am I supposed to believe?

I sit down on the couch and curl up with a blanket and a notepad.

My thoughts are all tangled together, one story weaving into another, one lie weaving into a truth.

I just don't know what is what.

Scribbling as fast as I can, I write down everything that I know. Trying to find any way to sort out some facet of reality.

Aunt Cheryl has her story- that it was always Kara and she is a dangerous person. That nothing she ever said when we were kids was the truth. She was the only one who knew our family back then, her version would be the closest thing to the truth. If Aunt Cheryl is right, then I should be handing over the letters to the police and getting protection for when Kara comes back. I'm sure another manhunt would be out there for her, especially if there are two other victims. Which, admittedly, I feel horrifically guilty about. If I had read the letters earlier or at least handed them straight to the police, then those two might still be alive- if she really did kill them. But I can't think about that now. Right now, I have to think of a way to save myself.

The more I think about why I didn't hand the letters over from the beginning, the more an idea keeps prickling in my mind. My gut instinct says it's because part of me believed her. There was, and still is, a part of me that believes that I am who she says I am. Not only am I scared to know the truth, but I'm scared of others knowing it too.

Which brings me to the next person on the list- Kara herself. Her version of our history paints me as the bad girl. I'm the monster, the killer, the manipulator, and any horrific name you can think of for me. On the one hand, she has a lot of reasons to lie- to clear her conscience, to pass blame, or if she is the monster- then manipulation and lies are part of the fun. On the other hand, I'm the one with no memory except for snippets of nightmares. And unfortunately for me, the snippets of nightmares have begun to make sense when I compare them to her stories.

I've searched the house a million times looking for any clues my mom may have stashed away before...well, before what? Before she died of an overdose, either on purpose or on accident? Or, when I murdered her without remembering?

Another uncertainty I will have to unravel, even though I'm not sure I want to know the truth. Then again, I don't want to know the truth about any of this. I'd kill for the chance to go back and live back in my self-involved existence again where I felt bad for my poor little life and didn't have to wonder if I was actually a murderer.

No clues have been left behind in my house, so Mom's secrets will have to stay hidden. I wonder if somewhere in the house is contact information for my dad. If there is, maybe he could shed some light on our family history. I dig through my mom's address book and her phone contact list looking for either his name or a name that I don't recognize at all, in case she wanted to keep him hidden. When I come up empty, I make a desperate attempt to rifle through her drawers and jewelry boxes, wondering if all I'm looking for is a small slip of paper buried somewhere. Like an 'in case of emergency' situation.

But I come up empty again.

I curl back up on the couch, slightly deflated with no help from my mom from beyond the grave. And the notes on my pad don't seem to be leading me anywhere. At least, nowhere that is helpful.

My mind is useless in my search for the truth, which is the most frustrating part of all of this.

If you can't trust yourself, who can you trust?

Certainly, not my family, which I've only recently learned.

Where can I go from here? Who would have any factual information about the past- something concrete that would help me put the pieces together?

A thought pops into my mind and before I can question if it will lead me anywhere helpful, I grab my phone and dial the number.

"Holden Lake Institute, how may I help you?"

I clear my throat and take a deep breath. My new relationship with Holden Lake Institute has been a tenuous one. It's been filled with legal and moral blame as it was her doctors who said she was ready to come home, but it was me who said I would take care of her and contact them if there were any concerns.

We all dropped the ball and while the lawyers and police have still been battling things out behind the scenes, I'm hoping that the doctors will see the bigger picture and decide that I do deserve the answers I'm looking for.

But it might be hard to get those answers when I can't tell them exactly why I need them.

I don't have a choice; I have to try.

"Hello, this is Kara Heston," I say making sure to keep my voice even and relaxed. I don't want them getting their hackles up thinking this is about the legal stuff.

"Oh, hello Kara." The voice on the other end of the line turns cool, so it's clear the receptionist is aware of our uncomfortable situation.

"I was hoping I could make an appointment to come in and talk with Dr. Pratt," I say.

"Let me transfer your call," she says. Before I can answer her, the call is clipped and I am put on hold.

I have to wait a while before I hear the grating hold-music stop and Dr. Pratt's voice comes on the phone.

"Kara, I have to say this is a surprise. But I think any contact is supposed to go through our legal teams," she says.

Dr. Pratt, as calm and professional as always, does not surprise me with her answer.

"This isn't about anything legal," I tell her. I'm starting to lose confidence, sure that Dr. Pratt is never going to let me talk to anyone at Holden Lake. Logically, it makes sense. They need to cover themselves and protect their patients. Emotionally though, I'm drained and I just need all of the spinning to stop.

"What's it regarding then?"

"I just...I need some answers and I think you're the only place I can get them." I hesitate before I continue, knowing I need to be honest but also aware that I need to be careful of what I say. No one knows about the letters except Kara and me. And if I tell Dr. Pratt, I'm sure it will open an entire can of worms that I can't handle at the moment.

"Everything is so confusing and...my own sister almost murdered me. She tried and thankfully failed, but she's still out there. I just need to know the truth. I need to know what's real, what isn't, and who Kara is. I've tried everything that's been recommended, and I'm even about to get brain surgery to help me remember. But before I do that, I'm hoping to find something concrete, something to help put the pieces together."

I'm trying to sound strong and confident, that I'm ready for the truth, but I'm aware that instead, I'm coming across as if I'm begging.

Which, I suppose I am. Especially now that Kara is coming back.

There is a long pause on the other end of the phone which makes me anxious. I don't have anything more I can say to convince Dr. Pratt about how much I need this. If she says no, then I don't know where else I can go from here.

"Tomorrow evening, after I've completed my rounds. I'll tell you what I can, legally, and what I know about your sister. But if the conversation turns to a legal matter, I will be forced to end the meeting. I shouldn't even be allowing this, but I understand your position."

Letting out a breath of air I have been holding in, I thank her before she quickly hangs up the phone.

I curl under a blanket on the couch and lay there in silence. Today I was supposed to have my brain probed and fixed. Checking the time, I realize that I'm already supposed to be in recovery in the hospital.

Now, I have to wait yet another day to find the answers that I need.

Kara could already be on her way.

She could be anywhere.

I reach down under the couch and feel around until my fingers lightly touch the cool metal of the gun, relieved to know it's there.

Chapter 4

Kara

It's like déjà vu- being back on a bus in the middle of the night. Running away from a murder. Getting off at one bus stop, hiding in the dirty and cold tiled bathrooms waiting for another, then hopping on to get to the next destination.

The trick is to make sure that I'm not traveling in a straight line- right from my home to Kylie. If I were to draw it on a map, it would look like a zig-zag pattern of a bus line. Up a little, down a little, wait a little then get on another bus line to do the same thing. It's harder to catch a moving target.

Which is why Kylie doesn't stand a chance this time.

I've sent her the letters and hopefully scared her enough that she has been living on the edge since the first one. But what can she even do about it?

She doesn't know when I'm coming back or how I'm coming back. But after the last letter, I'm sure she is aware that I am coming back. I may have been a little...aggressive in the last one. I was just so mad. So mad at everyone.

Especially Kylie and her perfect existence. Living in her house with all that money, all that freedom, a spoiled past behind her, and whatever future she wants in front of her.

With a hood pulled over my head, I lean against the chilly bus window, watching the world slip past me.

The first time I escaped, I felt an anxious excitement inside of me. I had a future, a life to head towards. The world was finally at my fingertips instead of hers. What did I want to be? Where did I want to end up? Who was the person I wanted to invent?

According to my ID in my wallet, I am still the invented version of myself, but I won't be keeping that for long either.

I may not have started this journey home with a plan, but I have one now.

"Wow, what a shame, I was looking forward to the documentary."

The person next to me begins to talk, and I can't quite tell if they are speaking to me or not. Social cues are still a problem for me, or I wouldn't have had to stick keys in Adam's throat.

I slide a glance over to the passenger next to me, who seems to be highly interested in what he is reading.

Looking down at the paper, my heart begins to hammer, pumping a rush of blood through my ears.

I pull the hood tighter over my face, trying to block as much as I can. Though I know with the hair and the glasses I wear, I still hardly look recognizable. Even my coworkers never put together the pieces of who I really am.

But with the picture of her staring up at me, a smudgy black-and-white image, I can't be sure this man won't see through my mask.

I try reading it over his shoulder, trying to find out what the latest news on Kylie is, but the way he's holding it makes only part of the article visible.

I clear my throat and take the risk. I have to know what's happening to place her picture so big right in front of me.

I clear my throat. "Is that the girl getting the brain surgery?" I ask, keeping my voice as even as possible.

He sighs and shakes his head. "Not anymore. She canceled the operation. Or, well, postponed."

My body stiffens and I do my best to stifle a smirk.

"She did what?" I don't mean the words to come out as aggressively as they do but I can't help it.

He gives me a sideways look but seems eager to have someone to talk to so he ignores my comment and continues.

"Says here that she has some personal things to work through. That her journey will be documented either way. It's a shame too because I was looking forward to the medical breakthrough that was about to happen."

I ignore the part about her being some medical hero. She wasn't going to be a hero; she was going to be a coward.

"Does it say what her 'personal' issues were? Does it say what will be documented?"

He shakes his head.

"No. But I imagine that poor girl has so much to deal with. First, her mother dies by overdose- a possible suicide. Then she takes her long-lost sister out of a mental institution and tries to build a new family. Only to have her sister try and murder her and then escape the police."

My hand grips the keys in my pocket tightly, remembering what it felt like to have them go through flesh and bone last time. It was a satisfying way to release the anger I had built up. And this man is causing that same flash of anger to hit white hot inside of me.

To tell me my family history is just annoying, but to hear first-hand someone paint my sister as a victim; this poor girl who needs the world to rally around her, it makes me feel the need to release the anger.

If I wasn't already on the run and surrounded by people, I could easily see correcting this stranger for his mistaken understanding of the truth.

But I know that will just end with a key in his throat as well.

So, I release them and take my hand out of my pocket, wiping my sweaty palm on my jeans.

"Do you think that's the whole story?" I ask.

"I don't see how the media could have gotten it wrong. Her sister was locked away because she was a danger to society. That poor Kylie should have just let her rot in there."

Before I can respond, the bus comes to a halt. The man looks up from his paper, finally out of his trance about my family, and stands to walk off.

It happens to be my stop too.

I don't need him to think I'm following him, so I wait a moment and let others shuffle ahead before I grab my bag and leave the bus too. The bus station is crowded, full of people pushing and irritated, desperately trying to get where they need to go. The man from the bus is in front of me, and I keep a safe distance behind him, needing to get lost in the crowd of people.

Chapter 5

Kylie

I haven't been to Holden Lake Institute since I picked up Kara to take her home with me. When I pull into the winding driveway, the impression I have of the place is still the same.

It's beautiful.

It's built for children, to help them grow and work through their problems and traumas. Anyone can see that, from the outside, this is a place of help and peace.

But a strange comment keeps popping into my mind. And it's one from Aunt Cheryl. The night that Kara tried to kill me when I'd been on the phone with my aunt, she had said that Dr. Pratt and Holden Lake Institute were all a part of the cover-up.

As I walk from the parking lot and up to the entrance of the main building, I have to question if Aunt Cheryl could be right about it. Is this place as peaceful and helpful as it seems? Or is there something more sinister that hides inside those walls?

A chill goes down my spine and I shiver in the fading light of the October evening. It's typical weather for this time of year, decaying leaves dripping off of the trees to land on the dying grass. The moon is rising higher and earlier than in the heat of summer which lets us all live in the dark that much longer every day.

It's in your mind, there is nothing scary about this place I tell myself as I pull my jacket closer around me to keep out the cool wind.

My own words ring hollow in my mind as I open the door to the main entrance.

If this place is truly so innocent, then how did Kara come out the way she did?

The lobby is empty when I walk inside, which doesn't surprise me as visiting hours are over. Most of the staff are gone for the night, just the main support and night staff beginning their overnight shifts.

Even the receptionist, an elderly woman I don't recognize, is packing her purse when I walk in.

"Hi," I say brightly, reminding myself of how I sounded the first time I walked into this lobby. Bright, hopeful, and full of nerves.

The receptionist makes a big deal of checking the wall clock.

"It's far past visiting hours," she says- ready to scold me for trying to come here too late.

"I know, but I have an appointment with Dr. Pratt."

The woman glances down at an open book on her desk, then shuffles around a few papers, before pulling a post-it off of the side of the desk.

"Ah, Kara Heston. Right, you weren't written in the book for obvious reasons." Her original scolding demeanor has turned frosty instead.

It appears I have quite a reputation around here. I don't even have to question why I'm not in the book, I'm confident it's because a Post-it can be thrown out and denied that this meeting ever took place if it starts to turn into legal matters.

"Right," I say but my smile has dimmed. I'm not here to play games any more than Dr. Pratt is. I don't have time for that.

I don't know what Dr Pratt's motivation for meeting with me is, but I'm sure I'm about to find out.

"Well, her final rounds should be over by now so I'll walk you to her office."

I follow the receptionist back to Dr. Pratt's office. It's funny how different this place felt during the day when I was about to meet my long-lost sister. Now, I'm trying to find out the truth about my sister who tried to kill me, and the feeling inside of me is one of anxiety rather than uncertain excitement.

Dr. Pratt is already sitting behind her desk, waiting for my arrival.

She doesn't smile when I walk in the door.

"Kylie, it's good to see you," she says but the words are hollow. I'm sure she'd rather be speaking to anyone but me. I'm sure she'd even rather be talking to Kara instead of me.

At least then she could have her own questions answered.

Still, she gestures for me to sit in the same chair I sat in the last time I was in her office.

I was unprepared the last time I was here. My world was newly in an upheaval at that point and I still had shockwaves going through me at the realization that I had a sister. This time, I don't have the freedom to let my world spin. I'm here, and I'm ready.

"I appreciate you meeting with me," I tell her.

She nods. "This is all off the record, we aren't even keeping a record that you came to meet with me tonight."

A little vindication surges through me that I've predicted that situation correctly. It gives me confidence that I'm strong and smart and I can handle this.

"I understand that. And I want you to know I don't blame you for any of this, but I have to know the truth about everything. Who is Kara?"

"I wish I could give you some new answers, but truthfully, what I told you the first time I met with you was honest. We hadn't had an issue with Kara in years. She had been pleasant, had no aggression, and had become somewhat of a mentor for some of the younger patients. Honestly, she was a model person while she was here."

Dr. Pratt pauses and her face turns a little darker before she continues.

"It has given me reason to wonder what happened to her once she was released to you. She had done her check-ins, and she was following all protocol she had been given, so what happened to cause her to hurt you and flee the scene?"

My stomach sinks when I realize that Dr. Pratt is blaming me for this. She has her own motivation for letting me have this meeting. Not because she wants to help me find *my* truth, but because she is searching for her own. Kara was her patient and the closest person my sister had to her for years after my family disowned her. Dr. Pratt doesn't believe my story, or at least, she doesn't believe that it's the whole truth.

There seems to be a lot of that going around.

"Everything I've said to the police and in interviews is the truth," I tell her.

She leans back in her swivel chair and I can feel her analyzing me. Part of me wants to get up and leave right now instead of having to defend myself. But the other part of me knows that Holden Lake is the last possible place I can search for answers.

"Tell me again, what exactly happened."

I take a deep breath and start to talk. I've given this statement at least a couple dozen times so one more won't hurt.

"Kara was angry, planning this for what seemed like a long time. She blamed me and told me I was the one who did all the things she was accused of. And she thought the best thing she could do to get over it was to get rid of me. I tried to support her, I tried to bond with her. But in the end, all she wanted was revenge for what she thinks I did."

Dr. Pratt nods but I can see by her face she doesn't quite believe me.

For some reason, that causes a flash of hot anger inside of me. I was nearly killed by my sister and it was because of Dr. Pratt's promise that she was safe to be outside of Holden Lake. Technically, the lawyers are right- this is all her fault. How dare she act as if this is all somehow my mistake?

"Is there a problem?"

She shrugs as if she's trying to brush me off- but I can see the wheels turning in her mind.

"No, this is the same statement you've been giving this whole time. So, is there something else I can help you with specifically?"

Her change of topic is swift and there is a part of me that still wants to defend myself, but all that would be doing is wasting my time.

And I don't think I have much left.

"I just need to know what she was like when she was here. I know what you've said but if there's one thing I can agree with you about is that she couldn't just have snapped out of nowhere. Which tells me that one of us missed something," I say.

"I can agree with that, one of us certainly did. But I don't know what other information you want from me. I've already described your sister and her time here."

I shift a little in the chair, aware that this is finally my chance, maybe my only chance, to get the answer I need.

"But what about before she came here? What did my parents say about her? I think that's what matters here. Because that's what she's angry about, that's what she wanted to kill me for."

Dr. Pratt pauses for a moment, clearly surprised at the reason I'm here- to find out about what happened in the beginning. I need to know where it all begins.

"Your parents said that she was violent. That she had killed a cat, killed a child, and a lot of other things. They said she was violent, aggressive, and manipulative."

"Is that a normal child you would take here? Someone who is supposed to be so dangerous? Based on what I know about Holden Lake and the impression your institution gives, that doesn't seem to be the type of child you take in."

Dr. Pratt nods.

"You're right. When she was first brought to us, that was not the type of child we would have taken in. We took children who needed more...mental support. Not that they necessarily would be considered dangerous to other patients though."

This time, Dr. Pratt looks deflated.

"Then why did you take her in?"

I keep thinking about Aunt Cheryl and her comment that Dr. Pratt and Holden Lake were all a coverup. I don't know what that means exactly, but I'm hoping that something Dr. Pratt will tell me, even if it's an accidental hint, will help me figure out what that would mean.

"Because I was new, I was naïve, and I was hopeful. I had just started working here and Kara was so young when she first arrived. She was furious at being left here and didn't understand why she wasn't at home with your family. So, I bonded with her. Quite possibly I treated her as if she were my daughter. Maybe I became too close and couldn't see the truth, to see the real pain and anger she was in. But after a lot of hard work, one day it was like a switch. She became the perfect patient, and I thought I had done it. I thought I had made the impossible, possible."

That's all it was? Just an ego attack that made a young doctor think she could perform miracles? That's what almost got me killed?

The thought nearly enrages me and I can't help it that my eyes flicker, just for a moment, to the scissors sitting in a holder on her desk.

"But you didn't cure her, did you?" It's phrased as a question, but it isn't a question. I want Dr. Pratt to admit that she's the reason for everything that has happened since the day I picked Kara up from there.

"I don't know how to answer that. I don't know what triggered her, I don't know the full story- only your version. But what I do know is Kara was just like any other child when she was here for at least a decade. Which is why I have to wonder, what exactly it was that you did to push her to this point?"

Dr. Pratt is talking in circles and not giving me any answers. I don't have the time or patience for this.

I grit my teeth and speak slowly. "What happened before she got here?"

A condescending smile crosses her lips. "I think this is where we have to end our little meeting. Anything else should be between the lawyers."

I want to scream the truth- that I can't wait for the lawyers to figure all this out and that I don't give a shit about what they have to say anyway. All I want to do is protect myself and save my own life.

But I can't say any of that. If I tell her, she'll undoubtedly call the cops, and I still don't know if I'm ready for them to get involved.

And in the end, that's what this is all about. Well, that, and stopping Kara before she can kill again. And before she gets another chance at me.

So, I mirror Dr. Pratt and stand from my chair. I thank her for her time and pause to look around her office for a final moment, letting my thoughts churn before I follow her out into the hallway.

I know what I need to do now.

Chapter 6

Kara

I wake with a start as someone shakes my shoulder.

Instinctively, I swat at the air, my defenses up, but my hands don't connect with anything.

"Dear, are you alright?"

My eyes snap open at the sound of a voice I don't recognize and I spring up, leaving myself dizzy and confused.

I crash back into the plastic bus station chair and it makes my teeth clatter.

"Oh, take it easy," the voice coos quietly as if I'm a child.

When my vision settles, I notice the woman in front of me, wrinkled and grey. I probably do look like a child in her eyes.

"I...yea...I just fell asleep," I stammer.

Sitting up, I try to straighten out myself, and my mind, from its fog.

"But you were thrashing, it looked like you might have been trying to scream," she tells me.

My body does feel sore from being so tightly wound; I stretch to release some of the knots in my muscles. I must have been having a nightmare, though I don't remember falling asleep.

"You look pale, do you have some water or anything?"

Automatically, I reach down to my bag and grab the bottle of water I've slid into the pocket. I take a long gulp and try to erase the dryness that has taken over my throat.

"There, that's better. Are you going to be all right?"

I nod, even though my heart is still pounding and my skin feels clammy.

"Are you here alone? Do you want me to wait with you?"

"No," I tell her, giving no space for her to argue.

She takes a step back and offers me a tight smile before she walks away.

My mind is swirling with what is false and what is real at the moment and I need a second alone to catch my breath.

In my dream, I was back at Holden Lake.

I was young, probably not long after I'd been left there. We were making crafts in the art room. Cutting colored pieces of paper and gluing them down to make a picture, splashing some paint across the scenery. My picture was one of Kylie and me playing under an apple tree.

"You used all the green paper pieces," said a boy who was sitting next to me.

"I needed it for the grass," I answered. I was simply sitting there, minding my own business.

"But that's not fair. You were supposed to share!" he whined.

I ignored him and kept painting and gluing. I wanted to send the picture to my sister so it had to be perfect.

Then there was a blood-curdling scream, and it looked like a cup of red paint had spilled onto my perfect picture.

"You've ruined it!" I shrieked and spun to glare at the boy. But when I turned, he wasn't the same.

His eyes had become dark black circles, and there was a wide gash on his head. Blood dripped down his pale, ghostly face to land on my perfect picture.

"The nightmares will never end," he said. I could barely understand his words through his suddenly grave voice.

I opened my mouth to say something, but before I could...he smiled.

The smile stretched wide, a comical mask in the place of his childlike face. But there was nothing funny about him. His hate-filled eyes stared directly into mine.

Blood, thick and deep red, started to pour from his mouth. It covered the table, dripped down onto my lap, stained my hands, and ruined my clothes.

But I didn't move, I didn't scream, I didn't even react. I just stared at the blood, mesmerized by the way it took over everything in its path.

That's the last thing I remember before the woman woke me up.

She had said I was screaming, but after I've relived the dream, I don't think I was.

I almost feel as if I was laughing.

Dreams don't always make sense; I know that more than anyone. When I was living in Holden, I had strange dreams like that all the time. Ones that felt so real, and should be terrifying, but in the end, they weren't either of those things. Once awake they fascinated me as I relieved them. Then, I'd let them slip back into the darkness of dreamland and would move on with my day.

But this one feels harder to shake than usual.

It's as if the boy's eyes are still on me, watching my every move. He's all around me, even though I know that he was just a dream.

I don't even remember a boy who looked like that being at Holden Lake with me.

It's Kylie's fault. Because of her, I've had to relive the horrors of my past. A past I have tried to outrun but I haven't been able to escape from.

I check my phone and see that my next bus is set to arrive so I slide the water bottle back in my bag and stand to stretch. I'll be home soon and finally be able to put all of this behind me.

I'll do the job right and truly be free.

I reach down to grab the strap of my bag and immediately jerk my hand backward.

It's covered with something sticky.
And red.
Quickly, I swipe my hands on my dark jeans and grab my bag.
I need to catch the bus.

Chapter 7

Kylie

“I really do appreciate your time tonight. I know we didn’t accomplish much, but just to keep painting the picture is all I can ask for,” I say to Dr Pratt as she walks me out of Holden Lake.

“If I could be more help, I certainly would try. Unfortunately, there still is client-patient confidentiality, and on top of that the legal issues that are tied with this...well, I hope you can understand.”

She doesn’t hope I understand. She wants me to go away.

And I will.

Dr. Pratt opens the door for me and I step out into the darkness.

“Would you mind watching me walk to my car?” I ask. “It’s dark and I’m just not familiar here. Never can be too careful.”

She weighs my question for a moment before finally agreeing with me- a dark area that you don’t know isn’t the best place for a woman to be walking alone.

Stepping outside onto the front steps, the door closes behind her. Her arms wrap around her body as if trying to protect herself from the darkness too.

I give her a small, appreciative smile, and take a step down towards the parking lot. Then another.

Before I quickly turn on her.

“Oh, I can’t even believe this! I left my purse in your office.”

Annoyance, then frustration, passes over her face.

“I’m so sorry, can I just run back in quickly?”

“No, you can’t. At this time of night, the place is on lockdown.”

I quickly hop back up the steps and move right behind Dr. Pratt.

"We have limited staff so everything at this point is on passcode."

Dr. Pratt quickly types in a number on a keypad beside the doorframe.

The lock clicks and she opens the door for me. I scurry back to her office and grab my purse, being politely embarrassed enough that she had to let me back in. I apologize profusely but that doesn't seem to erase the irritation from her face.

We go through the same routine we just went through moments before. She walks me out, I thank her for her time, and this time she watches me get all the way to my car.

I unlock it and slide into the driver's side.

I even go as far as to drive out of the parking lot and pull off to the side of the road.

After a few minutes, I turn my lights off and creep back into the parking lot, making sure to park where there are no lights.

I sit and watch, waiting for Dr. Pratt to leave the building. I'm in no rush, I have what I need.

Running the numbers through my mind again, I make sure to keep them memorized.

1405925

The passcode to the building.

Dr. Pratt has her secrets, and she's clearly going to keep them.

But from what I can tell, so does this building. And I'm about to find out for myself.

I HIDE IN THE SHADOWS, keeping my hood up and my head down, even though no one is outside to see me. But I've never broken into anywhere before and I know this is risky. Especially with the lawsuit going on, and the fact that I am about to do something highly illegal.

What choice do I have?

No one wants to give me the truth- just their version of the truth.

But like they always say, there are three versions of the truth. Yours, the other person's, and somewhere in the middle is what actually happened.

It's that middle part I have to find.

Dr. Pratt is hiding something and everyone else seems to think they know what happened- but no one's story is adding up. So, it's time to stop asking questions and start figuring out the real answers for myself.

I'm not going to hide behind the truth I want to see anymore, I'm going to face whatever it is head-on.

But I have to do it carefully.

Slipping my hand into my sleeve to hide any potential fingerprints being left behind, I punch in the code I saw Dr. Pratt use.

The lock clicks and I peek through the windows to make sure no one is coming before I push open the door.

It's quiet after hours, the lights dim and there's no bright hustle and bustle like there has been during the days when I've been there.

It definitely makes the place seem creepier when it's dark and I'm alone.

Maybe it's because I've illegally broken into a hospital.

Or I've just seen too many horror movies.

But I suppose it could be because my murderous sister came from here.

Either way, a shiver runs down my spine and I have to give myself a moment before I can keep going.

I let the nerves settle and I focus my mind so that I can slip in and out of the building as quickly as possible.

But footsteps begin to click their way down the hallway and I force myself to get moving. I can't afford to get caught.

The feeling of someone gaining behind me makes me move a little faster down the main hallway.

On a last-ditch idea, before I had left Dr. Pratt's office, I had memorized the old, yellowed fire escape map posted on her wall. Now I need to follow the map in my mind to get to what I need.

Just as I hear the steps behind me turning the corner, I get to a big metal door that I know will lead me to the basement and, according to the map, the file room. Pressing on the handle and praying the door doesn't squeak, I push it open quickly and slip through it, easing it closed behind me.

Considering the rest of the institution is bright and welcoming, I thought the stairwell leading to the basement would be the same- but it isn't even close.

Florescent lights flicker above my head in giant metal hanging light fixtures. It seems they've been hanging there forever. The stairwell itself is cinderblock with a thin and peeling coat of glossy tan paint splashed over it.

It's like I'm not even in the same place anymore.

If the stairwell is this creepy, I can't imagine what the file room in the basement is going to look like.

As I wind my way down a couple flights of stairs, a dark open gap comes into view and I'm sure I'm about to make my way into the basement. Grabbing my phone, I click on the flashlight, just in case I can't find a light down there.

My steps echo as I slowly creep down, feeling goosebumps rising on my skin. Basements are creepy anyway, but I feel like this one is ten times worse since it happens to be under a mental institution.

And it's dark.

And I'm alone.

And, of course, my murderous sister came from this place.

Immediately I feel like I'm setting myself up for a scene in a horror movie, though I think I'm already living in one. But when my feet finally land on the cement floor- I know I have to keep going.

My hand searches the walls but as I suspected, I have no idea where the light switch is. Not wanting to waste any more time, I plow ahead with just the light from my flashlight.

The basement is vast, dark, and damp from dripping pipes. Tentatively, I take small steps, keeping my eyes open for the file room I know is down here.

Small rooms branch off of the long stretch of hallway and I have to peek through every one of them. Even with the picture of the map in my mind, down in the dark, I'm disoriented.

Most of the rooms are empty, just four blank cement walls with nothing inside. One is a laundry room with washers and dryers. Another looks like a pantry of foods, canned, and packaged. A third room has a foul-smelling mop, long since discarded I assume due to the flies buzzing around it, with tipped-over cleaning supplies. Some of the rooms house storage- empty metal beds, flipped-over mattresses, a few abandoned toys, and an unsettling broken porcelain doll.

The deeper I get into the basement, the more I have to fight the urge to turn around and run back the other way and forget the whole thing. I'll just have to make sure I'm prepared for a fight when my sister comes back for me.

But I've come too far- and if nothing else, I know I'll never rest until I know the truth.

As luck would have it, I make it to the final room at the end of the long hallway, and of course, that is where I find file cabinet after file cabinet. There is a little relief that floods me, that I was right and the files are still kept down here and I didn't make this trip for nothing. But there's another part of me that becomes immediately overwhelmed by the number of cabinets there are.

I don't even know where to begin. All I can do is open the one closest to me and see what it looks like. After a quick scan, I see that these are all coded by last names.

HES is what I'm looking for.

I open each drawer, checking letters of the alphabet, knowing that each time I do I'm a little closer to finding the file I need.

Noises clang above my head and my heart picks up pace.

Are those footsteps I hear? Coming towards me?

I freeze.

If anyone catches me down here, I can't even imagine the consequences.

They could even think I'm Kara searching for my own file.

Wouldn't that be ironic?

Something drops and I hear the noise bounce through the basement.

Someone is down here with me.

My hands shake as I go to pull open the next drawer which doesn't slide open as easily as the rest do. I can't tell if it's because I'm shaking or because it's jammed. But I try again, and again, as I hear the swishing of water and the slam of a door.

Someone is down here doing laundry.

I'm determined- even if I get caught, I'm going to get that damn file.

Finally, the stuck file drawer slams open and I'm positive that the person doing the wash is about to race in here to catch me.

Quickly I scan the letters until my eyes finally land on the H's.

"Is someone here?" a voice calls out.

I hold my breath, and my body, still for only a beat, before I keep searching for the letters I need.

My eyes light up.

HES.

I grab the one that has a K and open the file to check to see if it's the right one.

Heston, Kara is typed neatly across the front.

For a moment I don't know what to do. Half of me wants to rip it open right there and pour through its contents. The other half of me knows that I need to get the hell out of there before I'm caught.

Stuffing the file folder up under my shirt, I peek around the corner of the door. I stifle my breathing to let the room go silent. With that, I can hear the person in the laundry room still working away.

I could wait it out, wait for them to leave before I make my way back out. But that leaves me running the risk of someone else coming down and catching me. Instead, I decide to take a page out of my sister's book and move as silently through the hallway as I can.

The flashlight will be a total giveaway, so I look down the hall and quickly memorize the path out of the basement and back to the stairwell. I shut it off with a wing and a prayer to whoever may be listening, that I can move silently.

Especially when I pass by the laundry room.

Apparently, I'm not as quiet as I think I am.

"Hello? Who is down here?" a nervous voice calls out.

I can't blame them- if I had to work in this basement I'd be just as scared if I heard noises rustling.

But I can't risk getting caught. So, with much less concern for the noise and more concern for getting out without being seen, I break into a run. My shoes slapping the ground.

"Hello? Who is there?" the voice echoes down the hallway.

I can picture them looking out the doorway, down the hallway to see the shadow in the darkness.

But by the time their voice hits the hallway, I've made it to the stairs which I take two at a time.

Once at the top, I slow my pace to not look obvious, but I still move quickly, back through the hallways, to the front door, and out to the parking lot.

I begin gulping in the fresh air, realizing that I don't know when the last time I took a full breath was.

But I got what I came for.
And I can only hope the answers are in there.

Chapter 8

Kylie

When I arrive home, I throw my keys on the counter and let my body finally lose its tension. Speeding all the way home, Kara's files felt as if they were taunting me from the passenger seat. Those pages stacked inside the worn manilla folder are the key to everything.

I drop the file on the kitchen table and take off my damp jacket, shaking out some of the chill that's settled inside of me. Grabbing a chair, I slide it from the table and sit, staring at the folder.

It's finally right there- the answer to who Kara is, why my life turned out the way it has, and who I am.

Shakily, I grasp the front of the file and begin to open it. But something inside of me makes me stop.

I'm torn between what I'm about to learn. Am I going to find out what I'm up against? Or am I going to learn that it's the world that should be afraid of me?

I just need a moment to catch my breath and let the nerves inside of me settle. I realize how badly I'm shaking and for the first time, I notice that my clothes are damp all the way through from leaking pipes in the Holden Lake basement.

I slide out from the table and make my way upstairs, deciding to change my clothes to something warmer and more comfortable before I dig into the folder. Hopefully, then the shivers will subside.

I take sweatpants from a drawer in my dresser and a heavy sweatshirt from where I had tossed it on a chair. My heart is racing and my hands won't stop shaking.

Get a grip, I tell myself as I sit on the side of the bed and take a sip of water from a bottle on my nightstand.

That's the last thing I remember.

When I wake up, I feel groggy, confused, and unsure of how I even was able to fall asleep when I had so much adrenaline coursing through me. Something scrapes downstairs, like a chair on a wooden floor, and suddenly I don't care how I fell asleep or why. The hair on the back of my neck stands up and my stomach plummets.

I don't have to have a twin connection to know that my sister has finally come for me.

It's time to finally face it- whatever that means.

As quietly as I can, I make my way into the hallway and flick the light switch.

Inevitably, the hallway stays dark. I flick it twice more, just to be sure, but I remain bathed in blackness. Peaking down the staircase I can't see the glow of light coming from the kitchen either.

The power is out.

She's turned it off.

Clever.

Having left my phone downstairs, I have nothing to help me navigate the darkness but my senses and my familiarity with a house I've spent my entire life in.

I have to hope that will work to my advantage.

Quietly, I take the stairs one step at a time, tiptoeing until I hit the landing to the kitchen.

The moon glows in the window, illuminating the room just enough that I can see she isn't in there waiting for me.

She's still playing cat and mouse with me.

I'm so tired of being the mouse.

Realizing I've left the gun under the couch, I grab a knife from the block on my kitchen counter. Just because I'm the mouse, doesn't mean

I can't bite back. But the knife is only useful if she hasn't found the gun already.

The house is silent except for a soft rustling coming from the living room. Taking a deep breath, aware of what, or rather who, I'm going to find, I head towards the noise. My eyes dart wildly from side to side, looking around every corner before I move, peaking in every shadow. But I know that my sister isn't lurking in the darkness, she's not hiding.

Kara is ready to face this head-on.

And I am too.

The fire is crackling in the fireplace, the glow of the flames the only light in the living room.

Standing in front of the flames, her back towards me, is my sister.

I hide the knife behind my back.

"I was wondering how long that pill in the water would knock you out for. I was getting bored waiting for you."

"You drugged me?"

She turns to me, a half-smile on her face, and I am just as startled as I was the first time I saw her at the institution.

It's like looking in a mirror.

"At this point, you're surprised I would do that? That's kind of cute-you being so naïve I mean. Did you think the letters were a joke or something? Did you think I didn't mean it when I said I was coming back for you?"

"I knew you meant what you wrote in your letters. All of it. I knew you'd be back."

Kara turns all the way to face me and holds up the file for me to see.

"Was this your plan? This was all you had? To get my file and try to figure it out yourself? That's not much preparation." Her condescending tone frustrates me more than it should.

I reach towards her and try to grab the file. I feel protective of it-like I need to have it. Even though it's too late to read it.

She dangles it for a moment before she yanks it away from me and I stumble.

Her laughter sounds exactly like mine. At least I think so, I can't seem to remember the last time I laughed.

"You know what? I've looked through this file, and I have to say-there is a lot in here that I didn't quite remember."

Kara steps toward me, and I step away. This feels exactly like it did the last time I squared off with her. Although this time I know she won't hesitate to kill me. I know there's no talking her off the ledge.

"What didn't you remember?" I ask, trying to bide my time.

She opens the file and pulls out one sheet of paper.

"I think this is what you're looking for," she tells me.

This time she doesn't dangle it in front of me but thrusts the loose sheet towards me.

Hesitantly, I take it.

"You should read it out loud Sister."

Slipping the hidden knife into the back of the waistband of my sweatpants, I hold the paper with shaking hands.

It's session notes from Dr. Pratt.

"Kara has recently been displaying delusions of grandeur, in this case, she believes she is her twin sister Kylie. Under this belief, Kara's actions have settled, her aggressions have become non-existent, and she has become a pleasant patient with no current issues. This raises a question, would it be possible, or ethical, to let Kara believe she has the behavior and personality of her sister, in order to help her forget the violence of what she's done in her past? Would letting her believe her delusions prevent her from harming anyone in the future?"

I look up at my sister, her eyes trained on the flames that are licking the fireplace logs.

I read the notes again to myself but I don't think I fully understand what I'm reading.

The room stays silent for a long moment before Kara speaks again.

"You should see the notes that were written about me before that one. They could write a whole novel about me. And I'm sure that Dr. Pratt was aiming to do something like that. It's as if she was fascinated with me."

Kara looks up at me again, and this time I see something different in her eyes. The blackness is gone, the emptiness has been filled.

But I don't like what it's been filled with.

It's evil.

"I don't understand, you need to tell me the truth," I demand.

Nothing in my life has made sense since the day my mother died, and I can't live another second in a life that doesn't feel like mine.

"The truth is, Sister, it seems I made a little mistake."

She takes a step towards me, but this time I don't step back.

"What do you mean a mistake?"

Kara grabs more papers out of the file and clutches them until they wrinkle.

"It is a shame you didn't read the file. But bravo in getting it. If you hadn't, I never would have known the truth either."

"Kara, fuck, stop with the damn games already! I can't take it anymore!"

All the calm in me has left and I can feel that ball of heat filling inside of me.

She nods to the notes in my hand. "After that session, Dr. Pratt tried something a little unique. It seems that my solution to being in the institution was to convince myself I didn't deserve to be there. I convinced myself I was you. And Dr. Pratt, she went along with it to a certain degree. She told me I was Kara, but she let me believe that my life had been yours."

Her words swim in my head and I feel dizzy.

If that's true, then that means....

"Dr. Pratt said you had been a model patient for years."

Kara rolls her eyes at me, clearly annoyed that I'm not understanding.

"Of course, because I thought I was you."

Suddenly, all the pieces of the puzzle snap into place at once.

The anger she felt towards me suddenly seems justified. She genuinely thought I ruined her life and took everything from her. Even down to the bedroom. Dr. Pratt had let Kara think she was me, an experiment gone wrong.

She had convinced herself that my memories were hers, even though they were so unlike my own.

Fact and fantasy had melted together until she was the one who couldn't see the truth.

"Dr. Pratt was right though, once I believed that, I never had another problem again. She made one little mistake though."

I snort. "Just one mistake?"

Kara considers this for a moment. "You make a good point- she made two. One is that she never taught me how to not be *me*. She only taught me how to pretend to be *you*."

Something in the air shifts.

I swallow.

"And the second?"

"She never told me what I was supposed to do once we were both out in the world. And that's a problem because there can only be one Kylie."

I know what's coming next. I reach behind my back and take the knife from the band of my sweats.

She's right. There can only be one of us.

No matter the time or distance, twins will always think the same way.

Even when it comes to murder.

I feel my knife rip through her flesh, just as hers rips through mine.

Hot blood pools out of my stomach and against my sweatshirt. Pain flashes through my body. It's a nightmare I've already lived.

She twists the knife, and I follow her lead and twist mine.

Blood sputters up into my mouth and I can't hold the thick liquid in. It drips from my lips and down my chin.

The pain becomes too intense, I can't hold on. The world spins around me as I crash to the ground.

My eyes drift shut, and my sister drops to the ground next to me. I have nothing left to give in this game, I don't know if I can survive this time. I crack my eye open and turn my head to see my sister, lying next to me, blood coming from her mouth too. She's looking right back at me.

I close my eyes, and just pray that I can hold on. I pray that somehow, I will make it out of this alive.

"Goodbye, Sister."

Chapter 9

Kylie

The cameras are bright in my eyes, and I never imagined the heat would be so intense while I sit underneath them.

A person from makeup is dabbing some of the beads of sweat on my forehead and putting on fresh powder for me in a hurry as a man shouts that we have only a minute until airtime.

"Are you ready for this Kylie?"

I nod.

Oh, I'm ready.

I've been waiting my whole life for this moment.

"In three...two...one..."

The room goes silent around me and the show's host smiles widely at the camera. Her long legs are crossed at the ankles, looking dainty and feminine.

I cross mine, making myself a mirror to her.

Social cues are still a challenge for me.

"Kylie, thank you so much for coming on the show tonight. We know a lot of people have been fighting for your attention and of course, we appreciate you deciding that our news program should be the first you speak to."

"I'm thankful to be here and am eager to tell my story to the world."

She is right, since my sister's death, I have been getting contacted by every news show, crime special, podcaster, and author all fighting to get to tell my story.

But I've decided, I'm taking control of my life. I'll be the one who tells my story.

The woman turns to the camera again.

"If you haven't heard of this brave woman's journey, then you are about to hear from the face of inspiration. Kylie, first, we'd all like to say how relieved we are to know that after everything that's happened, you are finally safe. Though we do want to send condolences on the passing of your twin sister."

I nod, as I know I'm supposed to do. "It's been difficult. Painful. When I think of it all, the time she had to spend locked away, she couldn't have been getting the help she truly needed. Not when the moment she came home, she did what she did."

"Now, she eluded the police the first time she attacked you. Did you always feel she was going to come back and try again?"

I sigh, letting my eyes drop to my lap before answering the question. "I was always afraid she would. I hoped she would simply move on with her life and start over somewhere new. And she did- but then she murdered those two other people. I just feel so awful. If she had gotten the help she needed, had gotten the true therapy, or even been put into another institution...those people would still be alive. And so would she."

The interviewer is nodding along, sympathetic to the sadness in my voice.

"It must have been extremely difficult, to have to kill your sister in self-defense. It was you or her, did you know one of you wouldn't make it out of the fight alive."

"That's not something that crossed my mind. I didn't want to kill Kara; she was my sister. But I knew I had to kill her. It was survival instincts. I didn't want to die, but I didn't want for her to die either."

Even with the heat of the lights, the thrum of the excitement of the camera, and the lies I'm telling- my heart rate hasn't picked up speed once.

I'm impressed with myself.

"The strength, the bravery it took, I can't even imagine being in your shoes. What the world wants to know next is, what about the documentary? The brain surgery?"

I reach over to the glass table and pick up my glass of water, taking a sip. The pause fills the air and I know that this is the question everyone has been anticipating. My hand doesn't even shake as I put the water back down. It just lands silently, glass on glass, while the whole room waits for me.

"At this time, I don't think that it's in my best interest to have the surgery. The purpose of it was to restore lost memories, a life that had been blank to me. But now that my sister is dead, it's time for me to move forward in my life. Not look backward."

"It's why they say the rearview mirror is so small, but the windshield is so big."

I smile, hoping it looks kind and not emotionless.

"This is true. And I am looking forward to that. Instead of the surgery being documented, I do have some exciting news. I'll be doing a tell-all book, the truth about my sister. The truth that no one knows. And I will also be doing a special with the film crew, documenting my survival from my twin sister."

"It's truly remarkable, after all you have been through, that you remain in positive spirits and are looking ahead to your future."

"This is the first time in my life I feel I've been able to look ahead. I've spent years with questions and confusion, a darkness hanging above my head. But now, it's as if all of that is finally gone. I'm free."

"You've had all of your questions answered? I feel like I would still have a million," she says with a little laugh.

I don't like her laugh. It grates on my nerves and I take a deep breath to stop the bubble of heat that is forming in the pit of my stomach.

"I don't have all the answers. I don't think I ever will. The truth died when my sister died. But I have accepted that what I do know will need to be good enough. I am not going to dig around in the past."

She is still nodding along with me, like a little bobblehead. It was nice at first since it seemed as if she was truly listening but now it just seems fake.

I hate it when people are fake.

The bubble starts to burn a little hotter so I turn my attention to the camera.

"I'm going to live life as if it started the day my twin died. I'm going to live as if I get to start over again. It's like a rebirth with her death."

The studio is so silent you could hear a mouse squeak if you tried.

After a moment, the woman clears her throat and gives herself a shake, like she has to remind herself she is still recording. Her face has gone a little pale.

"We want to thank you so much for being here today, Kylie. And of course, we want to wish you the best in your future and your new outlook on life. Once all of this has settled down for you, what do you plan to do next?"

"I'm not sure exactly, but I don't think I'll be staying in the area. Maybe I'll move to somewhere sunny and warm. Maybe somewhere like California. I've always heard the weather is the best there."

"Cut!" someone yells after a long pause.

I stand from my chair as someone comes to quickly unravel me from the microphone.

"Thank you for having me," I tell the host, making sure to not forget my manners.

The woman's eyes don't meet mine. She opens her mouth like she wants to say something to me, but she closes it instead. Giving me a tight smile and a nod, she walks away.

As I leave the studio, I feel the rush inside of me still flowing. The lights, the camera, the attention...I feel like I can't get enough of it.

Maybe moving away from here isn't a bad idea after all. And maybe California and its sun are just what I need to start a new life. Maybe my next step should be out to Hollywood.

After all, I have excellent experience being someone that I'm not.

Thank you, Sister.

Hugs and Kisses.

Kylie.

www.ingramcontent.com/pod-product-compliance
Lightning Source LLC
Chambersburg PA
CBHW021451150726
47989CB00001B/489